NAUGHTY HOLIDAYS

2016

By Nicole Edwards

THE WALKERS OF COYOTE RIDGE

Kaleb

Zane

Travis

Holidays with The Walker Brothers

Ethan

Braydon

Sawyer

Brendon

Curtis

Jared

Hard to Hold

Hard to Handle

Beau

Rex

A Coyote Ridge Christmas

Mack

Kaden & Keegan

Trey

Rafe

Violet

BRANTLEY WALKER: OFF THE BOOKS
All In
Without A Trace
Hide & Seek
Deadly Coincidence
Alibi
Secrets
Confessions
Bounty
Off Course
Chain Reaction
To Have and To Hold
Missing Pieces
Smoke and Mirrors

THE JAMESONS OF COYOTE RIDGE
Hot Chocolate Wishes
Rough & Dirty

AUSTIN ARROWS
Rush
Kaufman

CLUB DESTINY
Conviction
Temptation
Addicted
Seduction
Infatuation
Captivated
Devotion
Perception
Entrusted
Adored
Distraction
Forevermore

DEAD HEAT RANCH
Boots Optional
Betting on Grace
Overnight Love
Jared *(a crossover novel)*

DEVIL'S BEND
Chasing Dreams
Vanishing Dreams

MISPLACED HALOS
Protected in Darkness
Salvation in Darkness
Bound in Darkness

OFFICE INTRIGUE
Office Intrigue
Intrigued Out of The Office
Their Rebellious Submissive
Their Famous Dominant
Their Ruthless Sadist
Their Naughty Student
Their Fairy Princess
Owned

PIER 70
Reckless
Fearless
Speechless
Harmless
Clueless

PRIMAL INSTINCTS
Chase (Volume 1-3)
Capture (Volume 4-6)
Claim (Volume 7-9)

HEROES & HAVOC
(Sniper 1 Security, Devil's Playground, Southern Boy Mafia)

Wait for Morning

Beautifully Brutal

Without Regret

Never Say Never

Beautifully Loyal

Without Restraint

Tomorrow's Too Late

STANDALONE NOVELS

Unhinged Trilogy

A Million Tiny Pieces

Inked on Paper

Bad Reputation

Bad Business

Filthy Hot Billionaire

RULE

NAUGHTY HOLIDAY EDITIONS

2015

2016

2021

NAUGHTY HOLIDAYS 2016

NICOLE EDWARDS

NAUGHTY HOLIDAYS 2016

COVER DETAILS:

Image: © alyonaillustrator (166029479) | © dashadima (173735083) | 123rf.com
Design: © Nicole Edwards Limited

INTERIOR DETAILS:

Image: © kanate (22764858) | © angelp (166925466) | 123rf.com

Formatting: Nicole Edwards Limited

ISBN: (ebook) 9781939786692 | (paperback) 9781939786708

Check out these five-star reviews for *Naughty Holidays:*

"As always Ms. Edwards gives us a lovely little holiday treat." ~BookBub reviewer

"Heat up the winter cold with this amazing collection of holiday short stories for the Nicole Edwards characters you love and can never get enough of." ~BookBub reviewer

"Such fun to get to catch up with some of our favourite characters. Perfect little snippets into their lives." ~BookBub reviewer

Nicole Nation voted, and the winners for the 2016 holiday have been chosen! Come and see how they are heating up the holidays this year!

Alluring Indulgence: Ethan & Beau

A Holiday Getaway…

Ethan Walker is living proof that gratitude is the best medicine. Despite the lingering shadows of his past, he's got Beau by his side, making everything better. This year, Ethan intends to give the man he loves the ultimate gift.

Sniper 1 Security: Trace & Marissa

Early Christmas Present…

Trace Kogan has one Christmas gift that he wants to give his beautiful wife. He knows she's ready, and he is too. Now, it's time for some action.

Pier 70: Hudson & Teague

To Give and to Receive…

Hudson Ballard and Teague Carter are about to embark on their inaugural Christmas escapade together. Knowing Teague, festive mischief is right around the corner. Brace yourself for a sleigh ride through chaos and cheer!

Bonus: Letters to Lorrie and Curtis are included (originally published on Nicole's blog).

Dear reader,

Back in July, I asked the readers to vote on which three sets of characters they would like to see holiday novellas written for. I was so excited to see the responses. I had so much fun spending time with previous characters and seeing what they were up to. I hope you enjoy spending time with them as well.

Included in this holiday book are three novellas. In each one, you will see your favorite characters celebrating Thanksgiving, Christmas, and New Year's.

Much Love,

Nicole Edwards

Holiday Getaway

Ethan Walker and Beau Bennett

from *Ethan*

CHAPTER 1

"HEY, E!" BEAU BENNETT WALKER HOLLERED AS he skimmed the page on the clipboard. "Did we get that part in for Braydon's truck yet? It was supposed to be here today."

No response.

Beau looked up and around the shop. Hell. Ethan had been right there not two minutes ago.

"Hey!" he yelled louder. "Where'd you go?"

Still no response.

Beau tossed the clipboard on top of his toolbox and headed for the small office, where they kept the coffee. The place was locked up tight thanks to the frigid breeze that whipped through the large open metal building this time of year. The heaters installed in the ceiling were blowing warm air, but due to the sheer size of the place, they didn't help a whole lot.

He noticed the office door was closed and he paused momentarily. Very rarely did Ethan close the door. Usually only when he was taking an important phone call, which was extremely rare.

Beau rapped on the door lightly, then turned the knob. Hmm. Unlocked.

He pushed the door open to find...

"Holy God," he breathed out.

There was Ethan, sitting in his leather chair, his jeans down around his knees, his dick in his hands. When their eyes met, Beau could see the heat reflected in his husband's blue-gray eyes.

"I was wonderin' when you'd finally get in here."

Beau closed the door behind him. He flipped the lock for the hell of it. Every now and then, one of Ethan's brothers would wander in, and now was not a good time.

Ethan crooked his finger, urging Beau to come closer.

His legs worked without any instruction from his brain.

Nope, Beau knew his big head was not in charge right now.

When he was close enough, Ethan reached out and took Beau's hand, guiding it down to his cock.

"Stroke me."

It clearly wasn't a request, and sure as shit, that had Beau's dick quickly throbbing behind his zipper. As he leaned over, one hand on the arm of the chair so he didn't fall forward, the other around Ethan's thick shaft, Beau met Ethan's lust-riddled gaze.

"Like this?" Beau asked, his voice rough, quiet.

"Just like that."

And then Ethan kissed him. Beau couldn't move because he was holding himself up with one hand and jacking Ethan off with the other, so he allowed himself to be kissed, which was apparently what Ethan wanted. When Ethan's tongue slid into his mouth, he groaned, loving the feel of Ethan's tongue as it stroked his.

This was a surprise. Back when they'd first gotten together and then for several months after they'd gotten married, sex in the shop was a frequent thing. And now, after nearly two years of marriage, sex was still a frequent thing, but never in the shop. They'd settled into a routine. Morning sex was always welcome, whether they were still in bed, in the shower, several times in the kitchen while they were getting breakfast. Nooners occurred only on the weekends, mostly on Saturdays. Sex before and after dinner was hit or miss, depending on what Ethan insisted on making. And of course, nighttime was the most popular time of all.

But this…

Damn, Beau missed this.

Ethan bit Beau's lower lip. "Suck me. Get on your knees and put my dick in your mouth." Ethan followed his demand by sliding his finger over Beau's lower lip, then pushing the tip into his mouth. Beau sucked Ethan's finger as he lowered himself to his knees.

"God, I've missed your mouth," Ethan whispered when Beau wrapped his lips around the engorged head. "So fucking much."

Beau loved when Ethan talked like this. He loved Ethan's commands, the way he told Beau just what he liked, conveying all the dirty things he wanted to do to him. Yeah, needless to say, their sex life hadn't become stale.

Both of Ethan's hands cupped Beau's head, but he didn't use force, simply rested them there while Beau bobbed up and down on his dick, taking him as deep as he could. Of course, that only lasted so long before Ethan took the reins, pulling Beau down onto him, thrusting deep.

"So good," Ethan moaned. "So fucking good. I love the way you suck me. Your lips ... your tongue ... so fucking perfect. Oh, God, Beau."

Beau applied more suction, doing all the things he knew Ethan enjoyed, including using his hands to cup and knead Ethan's balls. He balanced it out, not wanting to push Ethan to the edge yet. The fact of the matter was, Beau loved this. Loved when Ethan got demanding, told him to go to his knees, then thrust his cock into Beau's mouth. It turned him on because it turned Ethan on. And what made Ethan happy made Beau happy.

"Fuck, baby," Ethan hissed. "Do that again."

Beau curled his tongue around the head of Ethan's cock.

"I fucking love your mouth on me, Beau. Fucking love it."

That was evident.

"You think I should come in your mouth?"

Beau nodded.

"Or you think I should bend you over this desk and fuck your tight ass?"

His ass clenched in anticipation and he let out an appreciative groan. He knew Ethan wasn't really leaving it up to him. He'd already made a decision. If he hadn't, he wouldn't have asked.

Another thing Beau loved about the man.

ETHAN WALKER WASN'T SURE WHAT HAD GOTTEN into him or why he'd come into the small office, hoping Beau would eventually seek him out. But that was exactly what he'd done, desperate for his daily dose of the man. He probably could've waited until tonight, after they'd gone home, had dinner, and cleaned up, but he honestly wasn't in the mood to wait.

The man drove him absolutely fucking crazy, and Ethan didn't even think Beau realized how much or how often he did it. The way Beau walked, talked, moved. Smiled, laughed. Every damn thing about Beau was a fucking turn-on. Hell, if he could keep his husband naked all the damn time, Ethan probably would. Or at least he'd make the suggestion anyway.

But this … the way Beau so easily submitted to him. Yeah. That. Was. Fucking. Hard-on. Inducing.

Especially because Ethan knew that Beau could be just as dominating, sometimes even more so than Ethan. Yet he wouldn't even question when Ethan told him to get on his knees and suck his dick. And he did it with fervor, giving Ethan more pleasure than should even be possible.

Which was what he was doing right now, and if Ethan didn't stop him, he was going to come in Beau's mouth. Although the idea was thrilling, he wanted to bend Beau over the desk and sink as deep as he possibly could into the man because he just fucking loved it. He loved being one with Beau, inhaling his intoxicating scent, feeling the warmth of his body, listening to the harsh sounds of his breath as he tried to hold back.

Gripping Beau's hair tightly, Ethan managed to pull his dick free from Beau's mouth. But he wasn't done with the man yet. Leaning forward, Ethan crushed his mouth to Beau's, kissing him as passionately and as desperately as he could. He continued while Beau deftly worked his jeans open, then pushed them down to his knees. Only then did Ethan pull back, patting the top of the empty desk as he did.

Beau was on his feet in an instant, taking his position over the desk, planting his hands on the scarred wood top.

"Fuck, that's hot," Ethan said, reaching around and stroking Beau's dick. The man was fucking huge, but he figured it came with the territory. At six six, two hundred and forty pounds, everything about Beau was big.

He stroked Beau slowly, up, down, up, down, watching his hand work over the velvety length.

"Gonna make me come like that," Beau whispered roughly.

"Is that what you want?" Ethan would certainly do it if Beau said the word.

Beau shook his head. "Fuck me first, then… Oh, fuck…"

Ethan tightened his grip around Beau's throbbing cock.

"I love when you do that."

While he worked Beau with his hand, Ethan grabbed the bottle of lube from the desk drawer. He had to pause momentarily so he could lube himself and work two fingers, then three into Beau's ass.

"Uhh … fuck, E…" Beau leaned over farther, attempting to spread his legs wider, but he was hindered by the jeans shackling his legs.

"Ready for me?" Ethan asked.

"Always … ready."

Ethan pulled his fingers out and replaced them with his cock, pushing the head past the tight ring of muscles, pushing deep into Beau's ass, watching as he penetrated his husband.

Husband.

After nearly two years of marriage, he still got hard when he thought about the fact that Beau had actually married him. Ethan hadn't even known his life wasn't complete until Beau. Sure, he'd known he wasn't exactly happy, but before Beau, Ethan had been content to put one foot in front of the other and make do with the shitty hand he'd been dealt. But Beau had changed everything. To know that he got to spend the rest of his life with the man…

Ethan groaned as he pushed in deep. "Don't move," he warned Beau. "Hold perfectly still."

Beau's enormous thigh muscles flexed, his biceps bulging as he prepared to do what Ethan wanted.

Pulling out, Ethan watched as his dick emerged from Beau's body. He pushed back in. Over and over again he did this, keeping a brutally slow pace, not only teasing Beau but teasing himself at the same time. And fuck if it wasn't incredible.

"You want it harder?" Ethan asked.

"Fuck yes."

Ethan slammed into him but pulled out slowly. He slammed in again, grinding his teeth because the pleasure was so intense.

"Faster?"

Beau nodded this time, breathing hard, his fingers clutching the edge of the desk, knuckles white.

"Want me to make you come?"

Another nod.

Ethan considered sitting down in the chair so Beau could ride him until they both came, but their jeans around their knees were going to definitely limit their movement, so he settled on gripping Beau's hips and driving himself home, faster, harder, deeper.

"Don't you dare touch your dick," Ethan growled when Beau started to move. "And don't you dare come."

He knew Beau would hold out, and Ethan definitely intended to make it worth his while, so he focused on fucking this man he loved with all that he was. He pounded Beau's ass until he felt his balls tightening, that incredible tingle igniting at the base of his spine.

"I'm gonna… Fuck…" He nearly exploded, but he managed to hold back, not ready to give up yet. "Gonna come in your ass, Beau. That what you want?"

Beau nodded.

"Then I want you to fuck my mouth."

"Oh, fuck, E… I don't know if I can…"

Ethan grunted as he came, his hips slamming into Beau's ass one final time. He knew he couldn't make Beau wait, so he pulled out quickly, then dropped into the chair behind him, grabbing Beau's hips and spinning him around to face him.

Not wasting a second, he wrapped his lips around Beau's cock and allowed his husband to face-fuck him.

"E … oh… Fuck, baby… Too much… Too good… Your mouth…"

Beau gripped his hair painfully hard as his hips stopped pumping, his dick pulsing as he came in Ethan's mouth. Ethan swallowed eagerly and realized he'd been practically clawing at Beau's thighs.

When Beau pulled back, Ethan noticed the fingernail indents in Beau's legs. "Sorry about that."

Beau looked down, grinned. "I'm not." He looked up again, locking his gaze with Ethan's. "And if you ever feel compelled to do that again… Let's just say I'm going to be praying for a repeat every single day."

Ethan laughed as he stood up. He wrapped his arms around Beau's neck, clutching the back of his head as he pulled him closer for a kiss. "If we're not careful, there's gonna be a repeat in about three minutes."

Beau chuckled. "Then someone really is listening to my prayers."

No, Ethan was pretty sure they were listening to *his* prayer.

CHAPTER 2

"E?" BEAU STEPPED INTO THE HOUSE, SET his keys and his phone on the table by the door, shrugged off his coat, then headed in the direction of the incredible aroma emanating from the kitchen. It was Friday, and not only was it the beginning of the weekend, it was the beginning of Christmas weekend, Christmas being on Sunday.

"In here, babe."

Beau made it as far as the doorway before he stopped in his tracks, his eyes raking over the sexy-as-fuck man standing shirtless by the center island. Unfortunately, he couldn't see around the counter to know whether or not Ethan was wearing pants, but knowing Ethan…

Ethan's blue-gray eyes lifted, meeting Beau's across the room. A sinful grin tipped the corner of his luscious mouth, morphing into a mischievous smirk.

"You don't usually cook when you're naked," Beau stated bluntly, hoping like hell Ethan was naked. The guy looked damn good in clothes, but without… Holy fuck.

Ethan stepped out from behind the island. "Not naked."

Beau laughed. Nope, technically, his husband was dressed, if a pair of silky black boxers qualified as clothing—which they didn't. Considering Beau had every intention of pulling those off in the next two and a half seconds, Ethan was as good as naked.

Good thing it was warm in the house.

"What're you doin'?" Ethan laughed, dropping the knife to the counter with a clatter before dancing around the island, trying to get away from Beau.

"You can't tease a man like that." *Jesus Christ.* Ethan looked good enough to eat. All that sleek skin covering solid muscle… Screw the food.

Ethan's eyes darkened, but his smile didn't disappear when Beau pressed him up against the refrigerator. "Tease you?" Ethan snorted. "I wasn't teasing you. This was a test."

Beau leaned in for a kiss, sliding his hands up the smooth skin of Ethan's stomach and chest. He wasn't sure which part of him grew bigger, his dick or his heart. Both had it bad for this dark-haired, smoky-eyed, sexy-as-fuck man. "Did I pass?"

Ethan shook his head slightly, pressing his lips to Beau's.

"No?" Beau took a step back and stared at the delicious man crowded between him and the stainless steel refrigerator.

"Nope. I thought for sure your attention would go right to the food when you walked in the door."

"Baby"—Beau pressed up against him again, sliding his mouth to Ethan's ear—"there ain't nothin' in this world that'll pull my attention off you when you're half-dressed. Doesn't matter where you are or what you're doin'. Food doesn't hold a candle to you."

"Says the man who eats five meals a day," Ethan teased.

Ethan tilted his head to the side, granting Beau better access to that sensitive spot at the top of his shoulder. He sucked Ethan's skin into his mouth, his dick pulsing when Ethan let out a rumbling growl.

"Why don't we press pause on the foreplay," Ethan suggested, though there wasn't much conviction behind those words. "You go take a shower. Dinner'll be ready in about ten minutes. Afterward, we'll pick up where we left off."

Beau slid his hand down inside those silky boxers and fisted Ethan's dick. "You sure you can wait that long?"

Ethan sucked in a breath and went up on his toes.

God, he loved this man. Loved all the little things that Ethan did. The random tests, the sexy underwear, the food… Somehow, Beau had gotten damn lucky landing this one.

"Beau…" Ethan's rough whisper was sexy as hell.

"What's that?" he inquired, continuing to stroke Ethan's dick while he simultaneously kissed and licked his neck. He kept his motions gentle and steady but firm.

"Keep that up and I'm gonna come in your hand."

"Mmm…" Beau trailed his lips over Ethan's smooth jaw. "Is that a threat or a promise?"

Ethan started thrusting into Beau's hand and he knew he had to stop or finish. Those were his only options.

The thought of spending a couple of hours ravishing Ethan's body later was the only reason he pulled his hand back. Knowing Ethan could potentially have a violent reaction to his ceasefire, Beau also took a couple of steps back, admiring the view.

"Fuck… You're such a fucking tease." Ethan reached down and grabbed his own dick, squeezing it.

Beau chuckled to himself. "I promise to make it up to you later."

"You're damn right you will." Although Ethan kept his tone firm, Beau noticed the smile that pushed in the dimples in his cheeks. Nope, no matter how hard he tried, Ethan couldn't convince Beau that he wasn't already looking forward to later.

Continuing to laugh, Beau left Ethan in the kitchen so he could get a shower. He'd spent the better part of the afternoon under the hood of one of Walker Demolition's work trucks, and he smelled like grease and oil. Not the ideal aroma when trying to seduce your husband, that was for sure.

Not that Ethan had seemed to mind. Then again, since they both were usually reeking of automobile fumes, it was possible that Ethan had become immune to it.

The thought made him smile as he headed upstairs to their bedroom. It'd been a long damn week and he was ready for a couple of days off. Although they had no plans for the weekend other than the usual Christmas festivities, Beau was sure Ethan would come up with something else. Something that would require them both to be naked.

He always did.

ETHAN SNUCK A PEEK AS BEAU SAUNTERED out of the kitchen toward the stairs that led up to their bedroom. He fought the urge to stroke the hard ridge of his dick while he admired the way the man's legs flexed with every step he took.

Damn.

So, once again, he'd only thought he could handle teasing Beau. The man had a way of turning the tables on him, which he'd done one more time.

Ethan exhaled, forcing his attention back to the task at hand. He knew he had about fifteen minutes to finish dinner before Beau returned. And he wanted to have it all laid out by then because this wasn't just any dinner. It was tonight's gift for Beau.

Well, the beginning of the gift. He intended for the rest of it to play out while they were naked and Ethan was moving inside the man. Or, you know, maybe after that. Yes, definitely after.

Still, he wanted the night to be perfect.

He gripped his dick, wishing for a minute that he'd bothered to put on pants after he took a shower. The silk boxers did little to restrain him, and the last thing he wanted was for the damn thing to try to peek out while he was messing with the grill. That wouldn't be cool at all.

The thought of what was in that envelope sitting right there on the island made his heart hammer in his chest. No, it wasn't the ultimate surprise, but it was something he didn't think Beau would be able to pass up.

He hoped.

Being that they were gearing up for Christmas dinner with the family on Sunday, they had tonight and tomorrow… No, scratch that. Tonight he had naked plans, so they had *tomorrow* to get the last of the presents wrapped, to cook the food Ethan had signed up to bring to his parents', and to pack. The last part was the surprise for Beau. Since they spent so much time focused on work, Ethan had splurged on a nice Colorado vacation for the week after Christmas, something to get them away from Coyote Ridge for a little while.

It had taken some time to come up with the plans. The idea had first been planted in his head during the Walker family reunion they'd had back in October. Someone had mentioned the mountains and he'd been sold. Spending a week in a log cabin in the Rocky Mountains seemed like the most appropriate way for them to get some time alone. For one, it was isolated. Not to mention private. Plus, they could spend all their time by the fire. Naked. The fact that there would be snow—something they didn't get much of here in Texas—was simply icing on the cake.

And there, when they were alone in the secluded mountain cabin, would be when Ethan would spring the *ultimate* Christmas gift on the man he loved. At least that was the plan. He hadn't completely worked out that part yet, but he hoped he'd come up with something. He was relatively decent at thinking on the fly.

Ethan stepped out onto the back patio and pulled the cedar plank that held the salmon off the grill, then returned to the kitchen. Good news, no dick burns. Bad news, thanks to the bitter cold, his nuts were trying to do their best imitation of a pair of raisins.

Beau was still upstairs, so he hurried to get everything else. Broccoli with soy sauce, maple-glazed salmon, homemade crescent rolls, and macaroni and cheese (from a box)—one of Beau's favorites, go figure—had taken little time to prepare. It was one of those meals on the go. Easy to make, quick to eat, leaving plenty of time for some naked activities after.

Five minutes later, he had the table set, the food plated, and two beers waiting when Beau came back downstairs. Ethan's eyes nearly bugged out of his head when he caught a glimpse of his near-naked husband.

He couldn't help but laugh. Not because Beau looked ridiculous—although the Santa boxers were a bit ostentatious—but because the man had opted to dress up the same as Ethan. Nothing but the boxers.

"Nice," Ethan said when Beau pulled out his chair.

Beau glanced down momentarily. "You like?"

"I definitely like."

"Well, then you'll really like what Santa has hidden under here."

Ethan chuckled, pointing at the table. "Sit down and eat."

"Yes, sir."

Without another word, the two of them made quick work of devouring the food. Since his husband insisted he was still a growing boy, Ethan was always sure to make enough for the big guy. Beau was massive, and he could definitely put away some food. The fact that he was solid muscle made his appetite that much stronger. Good thing Ethan loved to cook.

When he was finished, Beau leaned back in his chair and took a swig of his beer. "That was fantastic. I still don't know how you do it. I somehow manage to screw up frozen fish sticks and you can make this."

"First of all, fish shouldn't be frozen. Second … that's why I'm responsible for cooking," Ethan told him as he took another bite. While he finished eating, he continued to watch Beau, enjoying the fact that he was shirtless. He loved admiring the man.

"What time is dinner at your folks' on Sunday?"

Ethan wiped his mouth with a napkin. "Mom said three. I figure we'll show up around noon. Maybe one. Help her get it all finished up. They wanna open presents around five; that way the festivities don't interfere with any early bedtimes."

Since there were so many kids these days, they had to plan these events to coincide with the sleep habits of munchkins. This year had been a busy one for pumping out babies. The Walker family had welcomed Rhett, Braydon and Jessie's little boy, into the world on September 9th. Then ten days later, Kade, Travis's son, came screaming out. They'd all had barely enough time to catch their breath when Sawyer and Kennedy's son, Matthew, was born on October 7th. Add Kaleb and Zoey's boys, Mason, who was almost three, and Kellan, now one, along with Kate, Travis's two-year-old, and it was a full-on daycare center. Oh, and they couldn't forget Derrick, Ethan's cousin Jared's four-year-old boy.

Christmas was going to be a wild party, that was for sure.

Ethan and his brother Brendon were the only two who had yet to provide Curtis and Lorrie with grandchildren, and if all went well, that would soon change. Since Brendon hadn't yet popped the question to his longtime girlfriend, Ethan didn't figure his brother was going to beat him to the punch. Then again, he'd been wrong before.

15

"I'll take care of the dishes," Beau said when Ethan was finished eating. "Why don't you get comfortable on the couch. You know, lose those pesky boxers."

Ethan smirked. "I was thinking we could watch TV in the bedroom tonight. More room and all."

Beau's smile was wicked. "Great idea."

So, while Beau took care of the few remaining dishes, Ethan grabbed their beers, along with the envelope, and made a beeline for their room.

CHAPTER 3

THANKS TO ETHAN'S EFFORTS TO KEEP AN impeccably clean kitchen, it took Beau all of five minutes to put the rest of the dishes into the dishwasher and turn it on. He damn sure wasn't about to waste any additional time, so he took the stairs up to their bedroom two at a time, coming to an abrupt stop at the very top when he saw the candles burning and his husband sprawled out on the bed ... naked.

"Fuck," he groaned, remaining rooted to the floor as his eyes swept over six foot five inches of prime, beautiful man, laid out on their soft gray sheets.

"Hi," Ethan said with an innocent grin.

Beau wasn't even sure Ethan knew what innocent really meant. Which, as Beau had learned, wasn't necessarily a bad thing.

Leaning his shoulder against the wall, Beau continued to stare at Ethan. He was propped up against the pillows, remote in one hand, dick in the other. The boxers weren't anywhere in sight. He was pretending to be watching television, which would probably be more convincing if the thing was on. Nope, Ethan wasn't fooling Beau. His man was waiting for him.

Ethan's hand paused mid-stroke.

"Don't stop on my account," Beau told him, standing tall again, then taking a couple of steps into the room. "You know I like to watch."

"You do, don't you?"

"I definitely do." And to prove it, Beau didn't take his eyes off Ethan's long, thick cock as it tunneled in and out of his fist. This was a leisurely stroke up and down, up and down, the swollen head glistening with precum.

Ethan's eyes followed Beau as he moved closer. "I just realized I didn't make you anything for dessert."

Beau chuckled. Ethan was such a tease. "I noticed that."

"Well, I've got something you can have."

"Do you now?" Beau crawled up on the bed, lying alongside Ethan. "Don't stop doing that. I'm still watching."

Ethan sucked in a breath when Beau placed his hand on Ethan's stomach. He traced the dips of Ethan's abs as he let his fingers move closer to Ethan's dick. Beau brushed his lips along Ethan's shoulder, then rested his head there, still admiring the seductive hand job taking place between Ethan's legs.

Ethan's lips brushed the top of Beau's head, and Beau's heart clenched tightly in his chest. God, he loved this man. He loved everything about him. He loved his sexy, devious side. He loved the sweet, albeit rare, side of the man. He loved Ethan's ornery, grumpy side because, yes, he had one of those in spades. All in all, Beau loved every single part of him.

"Beau?" Ethan's voice was a near-silent rasp.

"Hmm?" Beau let his fingers trail down between Ethan's legs, gliding over his balls while Ethan continued to stroke himself.

Neither of them spoke while Beau gently squeezed and tugged Ethan's balls, letting his fingers roam down Ethan's thigh, back up, down the other. He kneaded Ethan's heavy sac some more, enjoying himself immensely.

"Beau?" Ethan repeated. This time he sounded strangled.

"Yes?"

"Suck me," Ethan said. "Put those sexy fucking lips on my dick."

That was another side of Ethan that Beau loved. The demanding side.

Beau kissed his way down Ethan's stomach, sliding his tongue over the rippling muscle, dipping briefly into his navel, then stopping to lick over the engorged head of his dick when Ethan directed it at his mouth. Of course, Ethan was going to help the situation along, because his other hand slid into Beau's hair, guiding him lower.

"Your mouth…" Ethan groaned. "I fucking love your mouth… God, yes… Suck me."

Beau did as Ethan wanted, sucking him deep into his mouth, sliding his tongue along the smooth, warm skin while he continued to graze Ethan's balls with his fingers. He could do this for hours. Beau loved teasing and tormenting Ethan, bringing him right to the edge, then backing off. The hotter he made the man burn, the rougher Ethan got. Beau craved that from Ethan. Loved when Ethan impaled him hard and deep, taking what he so desperately needed.

Ethan's fingers tightened in Beau's hair. "All the way. Take me all the way to your throat."

Beau did, fighting his gag reflex, and Ethan moaned long and loud. When he pulled back, Ethan pushed Beau's head down again. Beau obliged him, allowing Ethan to fuck his mouth in a slow, methodical rhythm. Beau worked Ethan's nuts, kneading them, tickling them.

"Don't make me come," Ethan ordered. "I'm going to nail you to the mattress first."

Yes, please.

Beau didn't slow down or speed up; he continued to suck Ethan's cock at Ethan's pace. Only when Ethan pulled out of his mouth did Beau move, climbing over Ethan and claiming his lips. For long seconds, their bodies melded together, their tongues dueling as Ethan held him, hands roaming over his back, then down into his boxers, where he squeezed Beau's ass cheeks.

"You want me inside you, don't you?" Ethan whispered as the kiss lingered, their breaths mingling as they fought for air.

"Deep," Beau confirmed.

"You want me to fuck you hard?" Ethan pushed the boxers over Beau's hips.

"Oh, yeah," Beau answered.

Ethan pulled back, meeting Beau's eyes. Beau saw the hunger swirling in the blue-gray depths.

"I want to suck you first."

Beau didn't hesitate. He managed to lose the boxers by awkwardly bouncing around until they were off, then crawled up Ethan's body while Ethan shifted so that he was on his back. Beau straddled Ethan's chest, then fed the head of his dick into that warm, welcoming mouth. He had to grab the headboard as he was assaulted by sensations. Ethan moaned, sending electrical pulses straight to Beau's balls.

Staring down his body, Beau took in the sight of Ethan swallowing him. Their eyes connected and held while Ethan did insanely delicious things to him with his lips, teeth, and tongue. The guy knew how to give good head, no doubt about it.

"Fuck, baby," Beau breathed, white-knuckling the headboard as he tried to hold his hips still. Ethan sucked him harder, and Beau's head fell back on his shoulders as he groaned, pleasure making him dizzy.

Without a word, Ethan continued to blow him, somehow remaining in control although Beau was above him, outweighing the man by a good thirty pounds at least. No matter when or where, Ethan was always the one in control. Well, maybe not always. There had been a few times…

"Fuck, E. Keep it up and I'm gonna come in your mouth." Beau rocked his hips, desperately trying to hold back. Ethan's mouth was too fucking good, and the man knew it was Beau's weakness.

He felt himself drawing closer and closer, afraid he was going to lose it.

"E… Fuck… Don't… Not yet…"

Beau was practically fucking Ethan's mouth, chasing his release, although he didn't want to come yet. He knew what Ethan was doing, but he was helpless to stop him, so he clung to the razor-sharp edge of heaven…

ETHAN WAITED UNTIL THE LAST POSSIBLE SECOND to pull back. He'd long ago learned how much Beau could take, and he fucking craved getting him to that point like a drug. He loved watching his husband, the way he bit his lip in an attempt to hold back. He knew Beau would come if he let him, but he also knew Beau enjoyed being fucked more.

He barely managed to buck the big guy off, sending him backward while Ethan got to his knees, grabbing the lube as he did. Knowing Beau was still riding that high, the need to come making his body twitch as he gripped his dick in his giant fist, Ethan hurried to slather himself.

"Knees to your chest," he commanded Beau, his eyes locked between Beau's tree-trunk thighs at the gorgeous dick in his hand.

Beau drew his legs up toward his chest, exposing his beautiful ass to Ethan's gaze.

"Stroke your dick," Ethan instructed while he lubed Beau's asshole by plunging two slick fingers inside.

"Oh, fuck, E!" Beau rocked against the intrusion. "Keep… That… Yeah… Ohh."

When Beau broke things down to single syllables, Ethan knew he'd succeeded. He continued to watch Beau's face as it contorted from the pleasure Ethan was providing. He added a third finger to the mix.

"Oh, shit… Fuck me. Need your cock inside me."

Ethan continued to work Beau for a few seconds while he stroked himself at the same time. When it was clear Beau was once again moving closer to the precipice, Ethan got to his knees, lined up, and pushed home.

"Yes," Beau hissed, reaching up and grabbing Ethan, pulling him down so that their mouths touched.

Beau was folded in half and Ethan was buried to the hilt inside his ass. He focused on the kiss and not the blistering-hot sensation of Beau's ass squeezing his dick. It was fucking heaven every damn time. He would never tire of making love to this man. It didn't matter if it was fast and dirty or slow and sweet, it was making love. And it was *so* fucking good.

Ethan managed to pull back a little, looking into Beau's eyes. "Lemme watch. I wanna watch my dick sink into your ass." Just saying the words made Ethan's dick twitch.

That was all it took to get Beau to release him. Ethan placed his hands on the backs of Beau's thighs and began rocking his hips forward and back. Slide in, slide out. Insert, withdraw. Over and over, he watched as he speared Beau's fan-fucking-tastic body. Ethan alternated between looking into Beau's eyes, then watching as Beau roughly tugged on his dick, then back to the glorious sight of Ethan's dick claiming him in the most intimate way.

"More, E…" Beau's voice was strained. "Need more… Need it now."

Ethan thrust deeper, harder, but he maintained the same pace. Beau's beautiful face was drawn up as the pleasure bordered on pain. He knew his husband was holding back, and he loved him more for it.

"You wanna come?" Ethan asked.

"Yes." Beau groaned when Ethan slammed into him. "Fuck, yes."

"You ready now?"

Beau nodded.

Ethan shifted so he had more traction and began fucking Beau with relentless precision, slamming into him, retreating, slamming home again. He sank balls deep over and over, his breaths rushing in and out of his lungs as the sensation became too much. Beau's tight ass strangled his dick, milking him until he knew he wouldn't be able to hold on much longer.

Beau was jacking off, his hand a blur as it moved up and down his shaft while Ethan continued to plow him harder and harder.

"Fuck, E… Goddamn… Yes… Make me come… Oh, God… Yes, yes, yes-s-s-s."

The second Beau's dick jerked and twitched, Ethan let himself go, coming deep inside the man he loved while Beau's cum shot over his stomach and chest. Damn, that was beautiful.

"God, I love you," Ethan told him, still trying to catch his breath while they remained locked together.

"Love you, too, baby," Beau whispered, as out of breath as Ethan was, his body hopefully as sated, too.

"Don't move," Ethan instructed, pulling out of Beau slowly. "I want to clean you up. Then we can sleep, and you can wake me up when it's my turn."

The smile Beau gifted him with reminded him of all the reasons he loved this man.

Less than five minutes later, Ethan had cleaned Beau, turned off the lights, blown out the candles, and was now wrapped in Beau's arms, their legs intertwined.

"I thought you were going to sleep?" Beau asked, his voice soft.

Ethan smiled in the darkness. "Can I give you your Christmas present early?"

Beau chuckled, the sound a dark rumble against Ethan's ear. "I thought you already did."

Ethan lifted his head and peered down at Beau. The pale glimmer of the moon shone through the blinds, allowing him to make out Beau's face. "Not even close. There's plenty more where that came from."

"Then that's all I need for Christmas."

"I was thinking something more along the lines of the two of us. Alone. Cabin. Mountains." With every word he added, Beau's facial expression changed slightly. "Snow. Making love by the fire."

Ethan let out an embarrassingly girly yelp when Beau flipped him over and practically lay on top of him. He stared up into Beau's soulful brown eyes.

"A vacation?" Beau asked. "A Christmas vacation?"

Ethan nodded. "Technically, it's an *after*-Christmas vacation. We leave on Monday morning, come back on Friday."

"Do I get to do dirty things to you while we're there?" Beau teased, brushing his lips against Ethan's mouth.

"If that's what you want." Ethan didn't care what Beau did to him; he was always on board with that plan.

"God, E," Beau mumbled. "Why are you so good to me?"

Ethan smiled as he pulled Beau's mouth down to his. "I think you've got that wrong. You're good to me, and I'm merely trying to ensure you stick around."

"Forever, baby," Beau told him. "I'm in it forever. You can't get rid of me, even if you try."

Ethan had been a dumb ass and tried to do that once, back before he'd admitted he had fallen in love with Beau. He'd learned a lot since then. No way in hell was he ever letting this man go. Ever.

CHAPTER 4

CHRISTMAS DAY WITH THE WALKERS WAS UNLIKE anything Beau had ever experienced.

Every year for as long as he could remember, he'd been invited to Curtis and Lorrie's to do the same thing they were doing today. Sharing a huge meal with their ginormous family and then indulging in laughter and conversation for hours. There were lots of smiles, lots of kids, and even a few dogs thrown into the mix.

Before the Walkers had become such a big part of his life, Beau had spent the holiday with his own parents. There was usually a meal, although not large and certainly not festive. His mother would cook for his father, make his plate, even serve him, while she left Beau to get his own food. Once they were finished, she would clean up after them all, and his father would insist that Beau go outside to practice, with him there to supervise, of course. Football was his father's choice for Beau's career, and that meant every day was a practice day. Regardless.

Then the Walkers had invited him over one lonely Christmas day. He'd joined them for supper, after having eaten with his mother and father, after having spent two hours running drills his father had come up with for him. He'd sat there, at their overly full table—both people and food took up more space than Beau thought possible—slightly uncomfortable, but that hadn't lasted long because neither Curtis nor Lorrie would allow it. Beau had been smiling from ear to ear before the evening was over.

And since that day, Beau had actually looked forward to Christmas, more so since he'd been married to Ethan. Although he'd spent most of his childhood hanging out with Zane, being absorbed into this family by friendship, it felt like more than that now. It *was* more than that now. Beau was married to Ethan, and with some luck, they would have a family of their own one day, and they'd create their own traditions just like Curtis and Lorrie had been doing for well over fifty years now.

"Hey, Bennett! Get your giant ass over here," Zane teased.

Beau glanced over to find Zane sitting on the floor while Mason and Derrick crawled around and over him like he was a human jungle gym. Without question, Beau walked over and dropped to the floor directly in front of the tree. Seconds later, he had two squirrely little boys crawling all over him, making him laugh.

"Presents," Mason declared, turning Beau's head so that he was looking at the rows of wrapped gifts beneath the artificial tree.

"What about 'em?" he asked, pretending he didn't know that Mason and Derrick were seconds away from becoming pint-sized shredding machines with no regard to whether the gifts were for them or not.

"Where's mine?" Derrick asked, bouncing up and down on Beau's thigh.

He had to do some quick evasive maneuvers to keep his nuts from being trampled while Zane laughed from two feet away.

"Uncle Zane looks like a trampoline," Beau hinted. "Y'all go jump on him."

"Yeah!" Mason and Derrick squealed in unison, then launched over to Zane.

"Y'all desperately need to have some kids of your own," Cheyenne announced from her perch on the couch above Beau's head. She giggled as though she just realized what she'd said. "I meant you and Ethan … and you know what I mean."

Beau turned and smiled at her. He'd understood what she meant, so he didn't bother to tell her that it wasn't that easy for them. They lacked the anatomy to make that happen.

"Of course I do," Beau assured her. "And I promise, we're working on it. Hopefully one day."

He looked up to see Ethan watching him from across the room. He was standing beside Braydon and Travis, who were keeping an eye on all the rug rats, including Kate, who had latched on to her father's leg, trying to pull Travis into the living room.

Beau winked at Ethan. He knew how Ethan felt about having a baby. They'd talked about it at length on more than one occasion. Although he'd admitted to wanting a family, Ethan had some serious reservations. He'd lived his life hiding who he was because of the hate he'd endured firsthand. He said he had no desire to have a child who would have to experience that because he or she had two fathers.

It had been futile trying to convince Ethan that they weren't living in the Stone Age anymore. Although it might not be acceptable everywhere, it was improving. Only backwoods, ignorant jackasses like some of those who still resided in Coyote Ridge would dare to spout shit these days. Most people in this small town wouldn't come up against the Walkers though. They couldn't say shit and not offend this family who fully believed that love was love.

So, Beau had made a point to bring up the possibility of kids every few months, in an effort to gauge Ethan's reaction. Ethan hadn't yet told him what he wanted to hear, but Beau understood. He understood a lot about Ethan. And he knew he had to be patient.

"Come on, Uncle Beau! We want presents!" Derrick shouted.

"Presents, Unca Beau!" Mason hollered.

"Looks like it's time," Travis said, dragging Kate, who was sitting on his boot, closer to the Christmas tree.

While everyone found a seat—a much more difficult task due to the fact the Walker family had doubled in recent years—on the couches, the hearth, even the floor, Beau and Zane went to work passing out gifts. Or rather, passing them to Mason and Derrick so *they* could distribute them.

Although the little kids' gifts included cars, trucks, dolls, and Barbies, the adult gifts weren't quite as tame. Everyone had pitched in for Curtis and Lorrie's present again this year, but they'd all agreed that each of the brothers and their spouses would only receive one present, picked out from the rest of them. For the past six weeks, Beau had contributed his ideas to each of the brothers. In turn, all suggestions were combined, then voted on by that group. For example, Travis's gift—as well as Kylie's and Gage's—was selected by Kaleb and Zoey, Sawyer and Kennedy, Zane and V, Ethan and Beau, Braydon and Jessie, and Brendon and Cheyenne. Because Sawyer was the closest in age to Travis, he was responsible for heading it up. (Not necessarily a good thing for Travis).

And down it went. Kaleb spearheaded gift buying for Sawyer and Kennedy, Braydon for Kaleb and Zoey, Brendon for Braydon and Jessie, Ethan for Brendon and Cheyenne, Zane for Ethan and Beau (God help them all), and last but not least, Travis for Zane and V.

Needless to say, everyone was anxious to watch this unfold.

ETHAN TOOK A SEAT NEXT TO JARED and his fiancée, Hope, on the hearth while he watched Beau helping to pass out the gifts. He'd been watching Beau with Mason and Derrick, and a pang of longing had speared his chest. Somehow he managed to push it away, reminding himself that now was not the time to be thinking about the things he didn't have. He wanted to be grateful for the things that he did have. Which, compared to this time a couple of years ago, was a hell of a lot.

"I thought y'all would be at the ranch for dinner," Ethan said, trying to make conversation.

"We will," Jared replied. "We figured we'd stop by here since it's still early."

"Did you go back to El Paso?" Ethan knew that Jared had promised his parents he would go home for Christmas. That had probably seemed a relatively easy plan until the man met Hope, falling in love practically overnight. Okay, not really overnight, but during the planning stages of the family reunion for sure.

"We did." Jared glanced over at Hope. "Hope was officially adopted into the family. She had to spend the day with Kaden and Keegan."

Ethan leaned around Jared, smiling at Hope. "I'm sorry."

Hope laughed. "It was interesting. But I've got four sisters, so I'm quite used to the antics."

"Hey," Beau said, coming to sit on the floor near Ethan's feet.

"Hey." Ethan shifted, ensuring Beau had enough room.

In true Beau fashion, he casually rested his arm on Ethan's leg. At one point, Ethan would've pulled away from the public display of affection, but over time, he'd learned that Beau was merely letting him know he was there. He wasn't trying to flaunt anything, and quite frankly, Ethan liked when Beau touched him. It'd taken a while to get used to it and to not automatically flinch. No, they hadn't progressed to kissing in public, or holding hands for that matter, but Beau wasn't complaining, so Ethan wasn't, either.

"Mom and Pop, we thought y'all should go first," Kaleb told them when he joined the group, Kellan in his arms.

Curtis grumbled, then smiled at Lorrie. "You do the honors, darlin'."

Ethan grinned. His mother was sitting on his father's lap, blushing like a schoolgirl. Ever since her near-death experience earlier in the year, his father had kept her close. Surprisingly, he'd managed to balance his efforts without suffocating her, though, which was the biggest surprise. It had been said, more than once, that a Walker man was nothing if not protective of those he loved. How Curtis managed, no one was quite certain, nor were they questioning it, either.

With Curtis's help, Lorrie hefted the large, flat box onto her lap and proceeded to unwrap it. Everyone watched raptly, waiting to see her response. It took a minute for her to figure out the first item she picked up, but finally when she pushed the power button, the sharp inhale was all the answer they needed as to whether or not she liked it.

"This is…" She glanced back into the box, then over to Curtis, then her eyes darted to Kaleb, then Travis and so forth.

"It's a digital picture frame," Jessie explained. "There's one for each son. Everyone downloaded their pictures onto a flash drive and those are inserted into the frames."

"We figured you had no more room for all the pictures on the wall," Zane explained, motioning to the line of frames along the stairs that took up every square inch of available space. "Thought maybe you could hang those up. Then you can see all the pictures you want."

Ethan squeezed Beau's arm when a tear slipped from his mother's eye. She was watching the slideshow on the screen, her smile growing wider with every passing picture. He knew there weren't that many pictures in his and Beau's frame, but he hoped one day that would change. In the meantime, she had some of their wedding, some in Hawaii from their honeymoon, and a few others to hold her over until then.

"Thank you," she said hoarsely, clearly choked up.

"My turn!" Derrick hollered, making everyone laugh.

"Okay," Curtis said with a grin. "Your turn, little man. Let's see whatcha got."

Nearly two hours later, all the gifts had been opened. There'd been tons of laughs shared because some of the gifts bordered on ridiculous, including a set of boob earmuffs, Weener Kleener soap, a toilet fishing game, instant Irish accent breath spray, and even a package of condoms that had stupid sayings on them. Ethan lost track of who got what, but he was now the proud owner of the Weener Kleener soap. Not too bad considering Zane was sporting boob earmuffs.

That's the way it worked in the Walker family.

"Y'all seriously are gonna have to get more creative next year," Sawyer said as he passed out coffee. "These are standard gag gifts."

"Says the man who decided fake poop was the best suggestion made."

Sawyer grinned. "Yeah, well… I was a little preoccupied."

Ethan watched his brother's face light up as he peered over at Matthew, sound asleep in Kennedy's arms.

Zane nudged Ethan's arm. "So, did you tell him yet?"

Ethan nodded. "Yep. We're all packed and ready."

"Need a ride to the airport?"

"We have to be there by six."

Zane nodded.

"In the morning."

Zane frowned.

"You volunteering to be up that early?"

Zane's nose scrunched up. Reid had turned a year old in July, but everyone knew that the little boy didn't understand what it meant to sleep all night. Still.

"We've got it," Beau told him. "We'll leave the truck there. That way we don't have to catch a ride back."

Zane looked sheepish. "I really can drop y'all and pick you back up. Just say the word."

"No, really," Ethan told his brother, "we're good. You get some sleep. I hear there might be another little one in your future."

Zane's eyes widened and his head snapped around as he sought out his wife. Ethan laughed. It wasn't often that he could pull one over on his little brother.

"Jackass," Zane muttered. "Just for that, I'm gonna go get the missus so we can work on another."

"You do that," Ethan told him, still chuckling.

Beau leaned close to Ethan's ear. "You 'bout ready to head out? I've got one last present to give you before the night is over."

Ethan launched to his feet. "We're headin' out. Gotta get up early. Thanks for the gifts."

This time Beau was the one laughing.

But he was also the one following.

CHAPTER 5

"BUT IT'S ON MY BUCKET LIST," BEAU whispered to Ethan.

They were sitting in the last row in first class as the airplane finally leveled off after a good twenty excruciating minutes of turbulence. It was just a damn good thing Beau didn't get motion sickness, because holy hell, it'd been one bumpy ride there.

"And like I told you before," Ethan stated, sounding slightly annoyed, "there is no way the two of us will even remotely fit in that bathroom together."

Well, Beau had tried. Joining the mile-high club was the first thing on his bucket list, but it looked as though Ethan was going to quash that one right out of the gate. However, Ethan did have an excellent point. No way would the two of them fit in that tiny bathroom. Maybe one day they could charter a jet—Cheyenne could probably help them out there—with a full-size bathroom on board. Then Beau could finally cross that one off his list.

Until then…

Beau shifted and plastic rustled beneath his butt. He lifted up and pulled the plastic-wrapped blanket out from underneath him. He looked from the blanket to Ethan and then back. He smiled.

"What are you thinking?" Ethan asked, his tone bordering on frustrated.

They'd been in the air for almost an hour with another hour and a half to go. Beau was bored out of his gourd. The flight attendants had already delivered their breakfast and picked it back up. Most people were napping, while a few worked on laptop computers, others watching the in-flight entertainment on the baby TVs mounted to the back of each seat. No matter their choice of activity, no one was paying any attention to them. It helped that the other two seats in the back row—across the aisle from them—were set several inches forward, not quite in line with Beau and Ethan's seats. The man closest to the aisle had his eyes closed, covered up with a blanket. The woman near the window was reading a book.

Beau unwrapped the red fleece blanket as quietly as he could—which wasn't easy with the crinkly plastic and the otherwise noiseless first class—and spread it out over his lap, then turned his head and watched Ethan.

"I know you're not cold," Ethan said, not even looking at him.

"I am, too," he argued, although, no, he wasn't cold. Plus, the thin blanket wouldn't do much to ward off the chill, especially since it covered so little of him. But it covered enough.

Ethan turned his head, meeting Beau's eyes. He held his husband's stare until Ethan finally smiled and looked away.

"There's a reason God gave you long arms," Beau whispered, careful to keep his voice low enough so that no one could hear.

"Why's that?"

Beau nodded his head to the small console between their seats. "So you can reach over that."

Ethan snorted, making Beau laugh.

Instead of pestering Ethan, Beau leaned his seat back and pretended to watch the television on the seat in front of him. He wasn't the least bit interested in any of the in-flight entertainment. Well, not unless Ethan was going to be the one doing the entertaining.

A good twenty minutes passed before Beau heard Ethan opening his blanket, then tucking the plastic into the seat pocket. He laid out the thin, drab red cloth over himself and then over the console.

Interesting.

Beau didn't move. Hell, he hardly breathed. And when Ethan's hand slipped down into his lap, it took every ounce of restraint not to suck in air. Instead, Beau propped his own blanket up so that whatever movement was occurring beneath it wouldn't be seen by anyone who happened to look their way.

Luckily, Beau had thought ahead and planned for comfort. The sweat pants he wore gave Ethan all the access he needed, and based on where his hand slipped, it looked as though he needed.

Beau had to bite his tongue when Ethan's warm fingers encircled his dick. He briefly looked down at his lap, ensuring there wasn't any visible movement. When he was satisfied that no one would be able to tell what Ethan was doing, he closed his eyes.

The impromptu hand job was exquisite. Mind-numbingly so.

However, when he'd come up with the plan, he hadn't considered how difficult it would be not to make a sound. He had never had to keep it down when it came to Ethan giving him pleasure. But here, he couldn't even breathe heavily or someone was going to figure out what was going on.

Rather than grab hold of Ethan, Beau forced his eyes open, then turned his head so that he was looking at the man. Ethan leaned back, also staring at Beau. They held one another's gaze while Ethan worked Beau's dick. Beau swallowed hard.

Nope, he certainly hadn't thought this all the way through. Not only was he forced to be quiet—far more difficult than one might think—he also had to worry that when he came, it was going to smell like sex.

He shook his head, trying to tell Ethan to stop. They were going to get caught.

Oh, fuck. Oh, fuck.

No way would these people not know that Beau had come. Not to mention, he was going to make a mess.

His eyes widened and he tried to mentally relay the message to Ethan. Beau wasn't sure he understood.

Then, Ethan did something Beau would've never in his life expected.

In one quick move, Ethan's head disappeared under the blanket as he leaned over the console, wrapped his lips around Beau's dick and ... sucked.

That did it.

With a rush of air from his lungs, Beau came right down his husband's throat.

Oh, and there might've been a little squeak, too. He couldn't be sure.

ETHAN HAD MANAGED TO SLEEP THE VERY last leg of the trip, roughly thirty minutes. He had even managed to stay asleep on the descent into Denver, which meant he'd been exhausted. Beau woke him when the plane landed. From there, they grabbed their luggage, retrieved their rental car, then set out on the hour-and-a-half drive from the airport to the cabin they'd rented in Breckenridge.

It had been a hectic day all around, but the second Ethan set foot inside the rustic, open living room with the floor-to-ceiling windows that overlooked the Rocky Mountains, every ounce of tension in his body dissipated. It no longer mattered that they'd been up since four thirty this morning and that it was now one o'clock in the afternoon—only noon in their new time zone. Or that this was going to be an incredibly long day.

"This is nice," Beau said, dumping the suitcase he'd brought in beside Ethan, then putting his arms around him from behind.

Ethan leaned back against Beau's hard chest. "Very nice."

"Is that a hot tub?" Beau asked.

Glancing at the deck outside, Ethan noticed steam coming up from the wooden box that, yes, definitely contained a hot tub.

"That's gonna be nice later," Beau said, kissing Ethan's temple. "Let's get the rest of the stuff."

Ethan forced his feet to move, following Beau back out to the rented SUV. On the way there, they had stopped at the grocery store and picked up everything they would need for the next four days. If Ethan had any say in the matter, they wouldn't leave this place until they had to head back to the airport early Friday morning.

Once they'd carted everything inside, Ethan put away the groceries while Beau emptied their suitcases and tucked them into the closet. Knowing Beau would be starving, Ethan set out a tray of cheese and crackers, along with some olives and sliced ham. As predicted, Beau followed his nose right to the kitchen and sidled up to the breakfast bar.

"So, what's first?" Beau asked, popping a piece of cheese into his mouth.

"Doesn't matter to me," Ethan told him as he stifled a yawn. He honestly didn't care what they did. He was merely grateful they were going to be alone for a few days. No work, no brothers knocking on his door, no cousins stopping in to chat. "We could spend the next four days naked if you'd like."

Beau's eyes widened. "I'd say that's a good idea, but I'm sure my nuts would shrivel up inside my body."

True. It was definitely colder here than it was in Texas. It was also prettier here thanks to the snowfall. In Texas, they had something more along the lines of *sn-ice* in the winter. It looked like snow, but it was really just ice with a little powder on top. That was in the rare instance that they received freezing precipitation at all. Some winters had passed when it hardly dipped below freezing during the day. So coming to a vacation destination with snow had been high on Ethan's list of things to do.

Beau popped a couple of olives in his mouth and grinned. "What d'ya say we take a nap? When it gets dark, we can spend some time in that hot tub. Where I can take advantage of you."

"Why does it have to be dark?" Ethan probed.

One blond eyebrow popped up on Beau's forehead as he hopped off the barstool and headed around toward Ethan.

Knowing he had just tempted the beast, Ethan slipped out of the kitchen and darted over to take cover on the other side of the couch. He would've been home free had he not slipped on the rug. Somehow, Beau managed to keep him from falling on his ass, but they did both go down to the floor in a tangle of arms and legs.

"I wanna bury myself inside you, E. It's been too damn long."

Ethan wasn't sure how long it'd been since Beau had topped him. For the most part, Ethan did the topping and Beau was the receiver. They'd mixed it up often over the years, but they seemed to have this rhythm that worked for them.

Didn't mean Ethan wouldn't welcome Beau to do with him as he pleased. He'd come to enjoy those moments when Beau took the reins. The guy was sexy as fuck regardless, but demanding Beau? He was a fucking work of art.

Ethan yawned again, which made Beau laugh.

"Nap first," Beau stated softly. "Then we'll play."

He was tired, but he didn't want a nap. Not yet anyway.

Rather than say anything, Ethan kissed him. He licked his way inside Beau's mouth, tasting the tang of the olives and cheddar. The temperature in the room heated drastically as they continued to make out on the floor. Clothes were worked off until they were both naked, their bodies grinding together.

"Let's get in the hot tub. Relax for a bit," Ethan suggested.

"Works for me." Beau nipped Ethan's earlobe. "But then we'll have to go out there again later, because I want you to ride me while we watch the sun set."

Well, okay then. Ethan could certainly wait until later because he liked the idea of that more than he could say. However, going out in the freezing weather, coming back in, then going back out, probably wasn't going to happen. So he had to come up with another idea.

"What d'ya say we find something to keep us occupied for a few hours. Then, I'll make you an early dinner, we'll eat, relax, and *then* we'll retreat to the hot tub." Ethan kissed Beau. "Where I'll ride your dick and we'll watch the sun set together. Sound good to you?"

Beau slid his mouth down Ethan's neck, his breath warm against his skin. "God, yes," Beau groaned. "In fact, nothing sounds better."

CHAPTER 6

ALMOST FIVE HOURS LATER, AFTER THEY'D TAKEN a trip back into town in order to burn a little daylight, Beau slowly sank into the warm water, relaxing as he did. Well, relaxing as much as possible when his dick was rock hard and in desperate need of Ethan. Although they'd done the touristy thing for a while, Beau couldn't deny that he'd spent every minute of every hour thinking about getting Ethan into the hot tub. He hadn't given a shit about any of the history of the town they'd selected as a vacation destination. Every step had reminded him that he wanted to get Ethan back to their cabin so they could have dinner and speed ahead to the sunset watching. Naked. In the hot tub.

Hell, he'd been so focused on it, he'd told Ethan he wasn't hungry when he offered to cook dinner before they headed outside. For the record, he seriously doubted Ethan believed him because, yes, Beau was always hungry. However, he wasn't only hungry for food, and his craving for Ethan had won out.

But now that they were here, Beau had to remind himself that he wasn't in a hurry, didn't want this to move too quickly—vacations were for relaxing, right?—so he sat back and waited for Ethan to join him. When he finally did several minutes later, Beau urged his husband to sit between his legs and lean back against him. Because a massage was foreplay, and that would definitely speed things along.

Not in a hurry, he reminded himself.

"You can do that forever," Ethan mumbled when Beau started massaging the tense muscles of his shoulders.

"I'm sure I could be bribed," Beau informed him, kissing Ethan's mouth when he tilted his head back a little.

"So what're we gonna do for the next few days?"

"Sleep." That's what Beau wanted to do. They had three more days where they didn't have to get up at the sound of an alarm clock. On Friday, they'd head back to the real world, but until then, Beau didn't want to do anything that was on a schedule.

"I like the sound of that," Ethan said, leaning into Beau a little more.

They got comfortable like that, watching the clear blue sky slowly turn brilliant shades of pink and orange before finally deepening to a dark violet. The hum of the jets and the pressure of the water against his tired muscles lulled Beau into a relaxed state.

"If we keep this up, I'm gonna fall asleep right here," Ethan said, his words thick with exhaustion.

"I'd be happy to tuck you in bed and wrap myself around you for the rest of the night if that's what you want." Beau would forego sex to hold this man if that's what Ethan needed.

"I recall someone promising to fuck me thoroughly."

Those words from Ethan's mouth had Beau's dick thickening as his blood pooled in his groin. They'd been together for nearly two years, and Beau still got turned on by every little thing Ethan did, everything he said. Hell, half the time, he walked around with a semi, his body primed and ready, just in case.

"Is that what you want?" Beau nipped Ethan's earlobe gently. "For me to slide up inside you and fill that sweet ass of yours?"

Ethan groaned. "I love when you talk like that."

Beau knew he did. He wasn't usually the dirty talker, though. Ethan was the master of that.

"I'm not sure there'll be any water left in this thing when we're done." Beau had spent a good half hour thinking of the logistics, which was another reason his dick was impersonating a granite club.

"What do you propose?" Ethan sat up and looked over his shoulder.

Beau took the opportunity to heft himself out of the water and onto the ledge behind him. The hot tub was tucked into the corner of the covered deck. Thanks to the walls blocking most of the wind, the steam was keeping the area relatively warm, although he didn't know how long that would last. If the wind picked up, he feared he would be a popsicle within seconds. Fortunately, it wouldn't matter in a few minutes because the friction between their bodies would soon generate enough heat to power the damn hot tub.

Ethan shifted on the seat, turning to face Beau. When his husband wrapped those fantastic lips around his dick, Beau sighed and reached for Ethan's head.

"I didn't expect that," he said, groaning as pleasure coursed through him. "Fuck if I don't love your mouth."

Ethan worked Beau's dick for several minutes. Beau finally had to stop him because, as much as he enjoyed Ethan's exquisite oral skills, he wanted to be inside him more.

From somewhere—God only knew where—Ethan produced a bottle of lube. He grabbed the bottle—which was warm, thank you very much—then proceeded to quickly slick himself up. By the time he was rock hard and ready, Ethan was already trying to impale himself on Beau's dick. With his legs still in the water, Ethan used the curve of the seat for leverage while using his arms to hold his upper body up enough for Beau to work his way inside him.

The angle didn't work at first, but Beau fixed that by shifting forward and pulling Ethan down onto his dick. A rough growl escaped him when the warmth of Ethan's body consumed him.

"Oh, yeah," Ethan moaned soft and low.

Beau didn't move, allowing Ethan to take what he needed. It was mostly dark, with the exception of the small colored light inside the hot tub. It provided enough glow for Beau to watch as Ethan lifted and lowered on his cock, taking him deep and slow.

"God, baby… That feels so good." Beau gripped Ethan's hips, guiding him down and up, the pace slow and easy. "This is fucking heaven. Being buried inside you…"

Ethan started moving faster, his ass gripping Beau's dick.

"Take over," Ethan commanded roughly. "Fuck me like you need me."

"Baby, I always need you. More than you'll ever know." Beau proved it by pushing Ethan off him. He guided him down into the water and toward the opposite side. "Lean over and grip the edge."

Ethan bent over, pushing his ass back toward Beau. He easily guided himself home, then pushed in deep. He leaned over Ethan, his chest to Ethan's back, as he rocked his hips. The water sloshed with his movements, despite the powerful jets circulating it.

Beau started slow, trying not to cause a tidal wave, but quickly grew bored with the pace. He could tell Ethan wanted more, so he began thrusting faster, driving in hard. "Fuck, E. You fucking drive me crazy. If you only knew how hard I get for you. How fucking bad I want to hear you beg for more."

"I'll beg," Ethan stated confidently, his voice deep and rough with arousal. "I have no shame when it comes to you. Fuck, I'll beg, Beau. Don't stop."

"Not stopping." Beau slammed home again and again. He finally stood and gripped Ethan's hips to hold him still. He fucked him harder and harder, deeper, faster, his fingers digging into Ethan's flesh as he held him still while Ethan locked his elbows to keep from being pushed forward.

The air was crisp and cold, but it did nothing to cool the heat that consumed him. Beau would never get enough of Ethan. Not even if they lived to be a hundred and did this every single day. The man made him burn, made him want, made him ache.

"Beau... Oh, fuck... That's good." Ethan pushed back, taking Beau deeper. "So fucking good. Don't stop... Gonna make me come... Oh, yeah... Just like that."

Ethan wasn't touching himself, which only made it hotter. Beau loved knowing that he could send him over the edge like this. His dick pulsed and throbbed, his balls drawing up to his body as his climax built stronger by the second.

"I'm gonna fill your ass, E. And when I do, I want you to come with me, baby. I *need* you to come with me."

Even as he said the words, Beau lost it. He couldn't hold back any longer, his release barreling down on him like a tsunami, waves and waves of sensation slamming into him over and over.

Nothing in the world felt as good as this.

Nothing.

AFTER THEY CLEANED UP AND TOSSED SOME chemicals into the hot tub per the cabin owner's instructions, Ethan made them a quick dinner of spaghetti and a homemade sauce he'd long ago perfected. He even tossed a few pieces of bread into the oven and made garlic bread. When it was finished, they ate in the living room in front of the fire Beau had started when they'd come in.

"Not a bad start to this vacation, huh?" Beau said when he set his plate—his second serving—on the coffee table and retrieved his beer.

Ethan did the same, then leaned deeper into the couch's arm cushion, sliding his legs against Beau's, who was on the other end of the couch, feet out in front of him, facing Ethan. "Not too bad. I'm only wonderin' how we're gonna be able to keep up this pace, though."

Thanks to the events of the last few days, plus all the traveling, Ethan was worn out. Now that his belly was full and his body sated from Beau's ministrations earlier, he was ready to sleep for a month.

"Did I wear you out already?" Beau teased. "I mean, you did turn thirty this year."

"Fuck you," Ethan said with a grin. "I only get better with age."

"Ain't that the damn truth."

Ethan watched Beau for a moment, their eyes locked together. He had a feeling that he knew what Beau was thinking. Probably the same thing Ethan was.

Ethan wasn't getting any younger, and although thirty wasn't geriatric, neither of them wanted to be too old to care for a baby when they finally got to that point. Beau was probably wondering whether or not Ethan had changed his mind yet. The last time they'd talked about it, a good six months ago, Ethan had told Beau he wasn't ready. He still had some demons to deal with, and he definitely didn't want to bring a kid into the mix until he felt he was mentally strong enough to handle anything that came his way.

If it hadn't been for Beau … Ethan didn't know where he'd be today. He had settled on being single forever, never having a family of his own. He'd been willing to be the world's greatest uncle and let his brothers have the kids. He hadn't even known he'd wanted more than that until Beau.

"I love you, E."

Ethan focused on Beau's face. "I love you, too."

"Thank you for doin' this." Beau waved his hand as though encompassing the room. "I think we both needed it."

Ethan agreed. It'd been a long year. It'd started with his mother's life-threatening illness back at the beginning. Then they'd made it through the hot summer months, which in their line of work was never easy. Of course, the entire family had been in a state of chaos since September when more Walker babies had started popping out left and right. Then they had the family reunion—a week spent at a dude ranch—back in October. It seemed there hadn't been much downtime.

In recent months, Ethan had found himself needing some time with Beau. Without anyone else around. Some quiet time where they could regroup, relax, and gear up for the coming year. Although he tried his best to hide it from Beau, he knew his husband saw right through him. It hadn't been easy watching all the babies being born and knowing that when the time came, and Ethan did want to have kids, they wouldn't simply be able to impregnate someone to make it happen.

Nope, in order for them to have a family, they had to decide on a path to take. There would be forms to fill out, agencies to talk to, income to prove. In order for them to become parents, they would have to prove they were capable, that they were deserving. Quite frankly, the idea of it was daunting.

There were so many options, and at this point, he and Beau hadn't really talked about any of them. Adoption, a surrogate… It was true, they had choices, but they were limited. And again, they had to prove they were worthy. That was the part Ethan wasn't looking forward to. He didn't want to be under a microscope. Didn't want people looking at him and deciding whether or not he was good enough. He had a feeling, when they finally did get down to that, he was going to buckle under the pressure. Fortunately for him, Beau was strong enough for the both of them.

Only, they had to get to that point first.

It boiled down to the fact that they needed to discuss it soon because Ethan knew they were moving in that direction. He knew how Beau felt about kids. The man would be an incredible dad, and Ethan wanted that for him. He wanted that for them both.

Ethan smiled at Beau. Hopefully, by the end of this trip, they could go back to Coyote Ridge knowing what their next steps would be.

After all, this trip was only *part* of the surprise he had in store for the man he loved.

BEAU WOKE UP THE FOLLOWING MORNING TO sun streaming in through the window and the scent of coffee drifting in the air. He knew Ethan was awake because they slept practically curled up together and the lack of body heat was proof that he was alone. He glanced at the clock to see… Holy shit. It was almost eleven.

Well, that explained the rumbling in his stomach.

Time to start the day.

Fifteen minutes later, after taking care of business in the bathroom, which included brushing his teeth and a quick shower, he emerged from the bedroom to find Ethan sitting at the breakfast bar, his iPad in his hand.

"Mornin'," he greeted.

Ethan's head jerked up quickly and the screen on the iPad went dark. "Mornin'. You want coffee?"

Before Beau could close the distance between them, Ethan was on his feet and heading for the coffeepot. Beau stopped him halfway, pulling Ethan up against him and planting a kiss on his mouth. Within seconds, Ethan's tension seemed to drain, and he wrapped his arms around Beau, hugging him.

"Coffee sounds great."

"How 'bout food?"

Beau's stomach rumbled his answer for him.

Ethan grinned. "Now that it's eleven, do you want breakfast or lunch? I could make breakfast tacos—sausage and egg or bacon and egg or…"

"That sounds perfect," Beau told him, studying the man. Why was Ethan jumpy?

Ethan laughed, but it sounded a little forced. "What sounds perfect? Which kind?"

"Both?" Beau answered, still watching Ethan before glancing down at the iPad.

Hmm. Ethan's sudden nervousness had to be related to something he was doing or something he was reading. Knowing Ethan would tell him in his own time, Beau brushed it off and took the mug of coffee Ethan handed him before heading over to the windows and peering outside.

"It's snowing." Beau wasn't sure he'd ever seen anything like this.

When they'd arrived yesterday, he'd noticed snow covering the ground. It simply hadn't been coming from the sky. It was easy to deduce that it had at some point been snowing, but Beau had hoped he'd get the chance to see it. Now he had.

"Been doin' it all mornin'," Ethan said from somewhere behind him.

Beau heard the clank of pots and pans as Ethan set to work making brunch. Because he didn't get the chance to watch him cook often, Beau opted to take Ethan's seat at the bar and admire the man as he effortlessly moved about the kitchen. The space wasn't quite as high-tech as their kitchen back home, but it was nice. He figured Ethan had checked it out prior to selecting this particular rental unit because he loved being in the kitchen.

"How long've you been up?" Beau asked, taking a sip from his cup.

"Since eight." Ethan glanced over. "I might've dozed on the couch when I was watching the news."

Beau knew that meant he'd probably crashed for another hour. The man was always in constant motion. He didn't usually sleep past seven, even on the weekends. However, he was known to take a combat nap at times in order to catch up on his sleep.

"Why didn't you wake me?"

"You were snoring so good," Ethan teased. "Figured you needed the rest."

Beau glanced down at the iPad. "Please tell me you weren't checking into work."

Ethan's blue-gray gaze slid over to the tablet, then back to the eggs he was currently cracking. "Of course not. I'm leaving that to Reese. Nothing we can do to help out right now anyway."

It took a second for Ethan's words to register. But then Beau remembered that Reese Tavoularis had been appointed to Jared's role now that Ethan's cousin was officially moving to Embers Ridge to be with Hope. Jared and Hope were in the midst of planning their wedding, along with counting down the weeks until their baby was born. Ethan had told Beau that Hope had thought she couldn't have children because of something doctors had detected when she was a teenager. Of course, having sex with Jared without a condom had disproved that theory. Since the couple was overly excited about it, Beau figured it wasn't a bad thing.

Of course, Reese had been a little surprised to find out that he was now in charge of running the day-to-day operations of Walker Demolition. But the guy was quickly learning the ropes. Beau didn't doubt he'd be fine. Not to mention, this was probably the best time of the year for them to take time off. Being the holidays and all, they were relatively slow.

"So, what's on the agenda for today?"

Ethan poured the eggs into the skillet. "I got the impression you didn't want an agenda."

Beau smiled. He hadn't said anything because he was willing to do whatever Ethan wanted, but he liked the fact that Ethan had picked up on it. "It's up to you what we do."

Ethan's dark eyebrows lifted when he met Beau's gaze. A sinful smirk tugged at his mouth, and Beau knew what his husband was thinking. By the time they made it back to Texas, neither of them was going to be able to walk. Not at this rate.

"I thought maybe we'd go out in the snow for a bit," Ethan said, as though he hadn't been thinking of the two of them naked the same way Beau had been.

"Yeah?" Beau sipped more coffee. "You wanna make snow angels or somethin'?"

"Or somethin'," Ethan echoed.

"Well, I say we eat, maybe take another nap … you know, the naked kind … then we can go freeze our nuts off out there and let you roll around in the white stuff. Cool?"

Ethan nodded. "I like where your head's at."

"If you're not careful, my *head's* gonna be inside you…"

Ethan's eyes flared with heat, and Beau knew he'd hit his mark. "Promises, promises."

"Damn straight."

TWO HOURS LATER, AFTER THEIR FOOD HAD settled and after Beau had made good on his promise, Ethan was holding his husband's hand as they walked through the dense trees that backed up to their cabin. The snow was at least a foot and a half deep, maybe more—Ethan wasn't really good at gauging that sort of stuff. Regardless, because they weren't familiar with the area, they agreed they wouldn't go far, but Ethan wanted to check it out.

Seriously, this didn't happen where they lived; he wasn't about to pass up the opportunity. He'd never experienced this back home in Texas. At most, they might've received a couple of inches of snow at one point in his life, but even then he wasn't sure. If it had happened, it would've been when he was a kid. His mother probably had pictures of him and his brothers doing something crazy with white stuff on the ground, but those pictures weren't the ones she was quick to show everyone. She preferred the ridiculously embarrassing ones, of course.

As they trudged along, Ethan quickly realized he wasn't a huge fan of this type of cold. The snow looked nice, but now that his bones were threatening to freeze, he accepted that checking it out from in front of the fire was a much better way to go. Did that make him a pussy? If so, so what?

Beau pulled away from Ethan, releasing his hand as he wandered a few steps away in the direction of another group of trees. He seemed to be looking at something, so Ethan kept his eye on him. Only Beau kept going, a few more steps, then a few more.

"Where're you goin'?"

Ethan remained where he was, eyeing his husband, waiting to see what Beau could possibly be doing. Neither of them had packed outdoor gear, so Beau was in a pair of Wranglers, with the legs tucked into his boots and his socks up to his calves. He'd gone full-on redneck today, and oddly enough, Ethan found it sexy.

Ethan's Carhartt jacket was plenty warm in Texas, but didn't offer nearly enough protection out here. As it was, he'd thrust his hands into his pockets because he didn't even have gloves.

While he continued to watch, Beau bent over, moving something on the ground.

"Beau? What are—?" Oh, crap. Before the words were out of his mouth, Ethan's brain processed what was happening as soon as Beau stood up straight, his hands molding something. Something white. Something frozen.

"Hey!" Ethan took a step back, jerking his hand out of his pocket and reaching blindly for a tree behind him. "Don't you dare, Beau Bennett. Don't you fucking dare."

"Beau Bennett *Walker*," Beau corrected.

That was so not the point.

As he tried to find cover, Ethan watched his husband stare back at him with a gleeful grin, a ball of snow in his hand. It seemed to be getting bigger and more compact the longer Ethan watched.

"I wanna give you the full effect of the snow," Beau said, his tone dripping with innocence.

"I *will* pay you back," Ethan threatened, leaning down and scooping up a handful of snow.

"You'll have to catch me first."

"Babe, I can outrun you any day of the week." That wasn't exactly true. Beau was a beast, but the man could run. He said it was from years of playing football. His father was always a mean ass, insisting that Beau be better than everyone else. Although his size gave him a significant advantage on defense, Mr. Bennett hadn't been convinced that was the right place for Beau, forcing him to do drills that would make him a prospect for several different positions.

In the end, an unrelated injury he'd received in high school had ruined Beau's ability to play ball and, in turn, ruined Ben Bennett's dream for his son. According to Beau, it was the best thing that'd ever happened.

Beau's arm pulled back and Ethan braced for the snowball that was likely going to hit him square in the face.

"Don't do it," he warned again, hoping Beau would change his mind. "Fuck."

He tried to turn at the last second but ended up with an earful of frozen white powder. He instantly retaliated, nailing Beau in the back with a snowball of his own. And then it was on. They chased one another through the trees, slipping out to launch another snowball every now and again. They probably spent more time on their asses thanks to the boots they wore, but that was okay, too.

By the time they were out of breath and agreed on a truce—in which Ethan managed to get in one more—Ethan's fingers were numb, his nose was frozen, and his stomach hurt from laughing so damned much.

"Let's take a hot shower," Beau said, taking Ethan's hand and dragging him back toward the cabin.

"We have to warm up first."

"That's what the water's for."

"You ever dipped frozen fingers in water? That shit hurts like a motherfucker. I damn sure don't want my nuts to endure that."

Beau chuckled. "Fine. I'll warm you *and* your nuts up *first*, then we'll take a shower."

Ethan gave him a crooked grin. "Sounds like a plan to me." No way was he going to say no to that.

8

BEAU RELAXED ON THE FLOOR BESIDE ETHAN.

After warming up from their trek in the snow, Beau had convinced Ethan to take a nap. This time, he'd been a complete gentleman, keeping his hands—mostly—to himself. They'd slept for three hours. When he'd woken up, he wasn't alone in bed, but Ethan was already awake, simply watching him.

Because Ethan knew him so well, as soon as Beau's eyes were open, Ethan was out of bed and on his way to the kitchen. This time, his husband had prepared grilled cheese and even pulled a bag of Doritos out of the cabinet. The man was too good to him. After they ate, Beau had convinced Ethan to lie down by the fire so they could watch the snowfall from the windows. Although he could sense Ethan was a little antsy, Beau had relented.

"What made you think of the mountains for a vacation?" Beau asked.

Ethan turned his head to look at him. He shrugged. "Wanted something different. Something we'd never done before. I was talking to one of Hope's sisters during the family reunion and she mentioned it."

"This is nice," he told him, leaning over and planting a chaste kiss on his lips.

"It is, huh?" Ethan turned back to look out the window.

"You're bored out of your mind, aren't you?" Beau asked with a chuckle.

"Absolutely. But I'm trying. This *is* what I wanted." Ethan laughed.

"We could play a game," Beau suggested, although for the life of him, he didn't know what game they could play.

"Yeah? Because we do that so much."

"Well, if you're wanting something we do a lot of, there's always…" Beau wiggled his eyebrows at Ethan.

"You're incorrigible."

"Yes, I am. Especially when it comes to you."

"So you've said."

Beau pulled Ethan closer. "Okay, so let's talk then."

"Okay."

It took a lot to hide his surprise, but Beau somehow managed. Ethan agreeing to talk? That didn't happen every day. Not sure if that was Ethan's way of simply appeasing him, Beau waited for Ethan to look at him again.

Ethan did more than that. He turned, planting his head on his hand as he stared down at Beau. The look in his eyes was unreadable, but Beau knew whatever was about to come out of Ethan's mouth was going to be important.

"I think I'm ready," Ethan said softly.

Beau frowned. Ready? "For…?"

"A baby."

All the air in Beau's lungs dissipated and he felt light-headed. His stomach did some strange twisting thing, and he fought the urge to laugh. Not because what Ethan said was absurd, either. Quite the opposite.

"A … baby?" Beau managed to choke out. "*Really?*"

Ethan's smile lit up his entire face. "Yeah. I want to have a baby with you, Beau. I want to have a family. I see all the pictures of my brothers and their kids… I want those. I want to fill that picture frame we got my mother with all the ridiculousness we possibly can. Taking pictures of our kid all the time, annoying everyone around us because he … or she … will be the cutest kid in the room. That's what I want." Ethan swallowed hard. "With you."

Unable to stop himself, Beau reached for Ethan, pulling him down and holding him close. He pressed his face against Ethan's neck and… Yep. He cried.

Like a girl.

And he didn't even care. His emotions churned inside him, and he couldn't stop himself.

Although they'd talked about kids, Beau had often wondered if Ethan simply told him what he thought Beau wanted to hear, trying to placate him. He knew Ethan was scared. The man had been traumatized when he was a teenager. He'd learned to fear everyone and to hide who he was. Beau knew Ethan worried about whether or not their child would have to face the same types of bullies simply because he or she had two fathers.

"Is that what you want?" Ethan whispered against Beau's ear. "Do you really want a family, Beau?"

Beau finally released Ethan and stared up at the man he loved. "More than anything. God, E. I… I love you. So damn much."

Ethan smiled, but Beau could see tears forming in his eyes, too.

Part of him couldn't believe this was happening. Although he'd hoped that Ethan would eventually come around to wanting kids, he honestly hadn't expected it to be this soon. They'd been married for almost two years, which seemed like a long time, but it didn't feel that way. Every day with Ethan was a blessing, and Beau was content just to have another and another.

"You know it's not an easy process, right?" Ethan said.

Beau studied his face for a moment. "I know. But, like your dad says, nothing that's worth it usually is."

Ethan's smile lit up again. "You're right. He does say that."

"Is that why you've been secretive lately?"

Ethan glanced down at Beau's chest. "Kind of." A shy smile formed on Ethan's face. "First it was this trip. I wanted it to really be a surprise for you. I wanted to have you to myself for a while. And yes, I wanted to tell you that I'm ready. So, I was looking up options."

"Like adoption?"

"Well, there's that. We could probably go that route, sure." Ethan met his gaze again. "But Beau, I want…"

Beau waited, knowing that when Ethan was ready, he would tell him what was on his mind. For the life of him, he didn't know what it was. Knowing Ethan, it would be something incredibly sweet— although Ethan would be the first to tell everyone that there wasn't an ounce of "sweet" in his entire body.

He'd be wrong, too.

THERE WAS A LUMP IN HIS THROAT that he couldn't seem to swallow past. Earlier, when he'd been playing out in his head how he wanted this conversation to go, Ethan hadn't considered he'd get choked up on the words. But here he was, staring down at the most incredible man in the world, wanting to tell him that…

"I want us to have *your* baby, Beau."

Okay. So there. He'd gotten the words out.

"Mine?" Beau frowned. "I'm … uh…"

Ethan could practically see the wheels turning in his husband's head. He let him toss that one around for a few seconds before he clarified.

"I was thinking we could get a surrogate. You know… Her egg, your sperm. Then we could have a baby Bennett running around. *Or…*" Ethan had found an article this morning, talking about a gay couple who had done something a little different. The idea was … intriguing.

"Or what?"

"Well, we could both donate sperm and … we could try for multiple babies at once. You know, two? I read that it's been done. They've fertilized multiple eggs with both men's sperm and… It's not a perfect science, but it has happened."

If Ethan didn't know better, he would've sworn there was a flash of anguish in Beau's eyes. Maybe he couldn't have kids? Although Ethan didn't want to know how Beau would know that.

"If you don't like that idea, I get it. I still think we should have your baby, though."

Beau's face was pale, but he didn't say anything, which really worried him.

"What's wrong?" Ethan finally asked when Beau didn't seem to want to talk.

"I … uh…" Beau sat up, then turned to lean back against the couch.

Ethan continued to watch him, waiting.

Beau took a deep breath. "I don't know if that's such a good idea."

Now Ethan sat up. "What? *Why?*"

Beau met his eyes, holding his stare. "I always thought if we went that route, we'd use your sperm."

"Mine? Why?"

"Because… Fuck."

Beau jumped to his feet and started for the bedroom before Ethan could get up from the floor. When he did, he heard the door to the bathroom shut, and none too gently. He went into the bedroom and stared at the solid wood door, completely baffled by what had just happened. Clearly he'd said something that bothered Beau, but what? Why was it a bad thing if Ethan wanted to have Beau's son or daughter running around their house? Beau would make beautiful babies. Blond hair, brown eyes. Ethan could see them now.

Ten minutes passed before Ethan started to really worry. He rapped his knuckles on the door, then took a step back. When Beau emerged, he looked as though he'd pulled himself together.

"Talk to me, Beau."

Beau shook his head. "I think we should use your sperm," Beau said, his tone flat. "And if you don't want to do that, we'll adopt."

Ethan didn't know what to say. "What? Why? I don't… Fuck, Beau. I don't understand. I thought you wanted a baby."

"I do," Beau said adamantly, his voice loud, his eyes narrowing on Ethan's face. "I just don't want *my* baby."

The words came out with such force Ethan actually took a step back. His own frustration was growing, and he got louder, too, when he said, "What the fuck? I don't get you, Beau. One minute—"

Ethan was cut off because Beau walked out of the room.

"Goddammit, Beau! Don't fucking walk away from me."

Beau didn't say a word as he went to stand by the window. Ethan followed, ready to lay into him again when he saw Beau's shoulders shaking. Was he…?

Ethan put his hand on Beau's arm and turned him to face him. Sure as shit, tears were streaking down his face. "Oh, God, Beau. Shit. Don't cry…" Ethan pulled him closer, wrapping his arms around him. "What the hell was I thinking? I'm sorry. I shouldn't have mentioned it. I thought…"

"I want a baby with you, E. I do." Beau held him close, not looking at him. "I just don't want any more Bennetts wandering around. You've met my father."

Ethan forced Beau back, needing to look in his eyes. "Your father? What the hell? Are you not thinking straight?"

"I'm nothing like him, E."

Exactly. "No, you're not," Ethan confirmed. "Not at all."

"But what if I bring a kid into the world and they are? I—"

"That's not the way it works," Ethan told him, cupping Beau's face and forcing him to look in his eyes. "You are not your father. And you're right, you are nothing like him. *Nothing*. And our kids would be nothing like him, either. That whole bigoted, hateful thing he's got going on… That's not hereditary. They won't be around him to see that."

Beau's eyes lowered. "My kid won't get to meet his grandparents."

"That's not what I'm saying, Beau." Ethan backed away.

"It wasn't a question," Beau stated, catching Ethan's eye again. "It's a statement, E. I'm saying my parents won't be allowed to see our son or daughter because I won't allow it."

Oh.

Shit.

Ethan knew that Beau hadn't gotten the closure he needed with his parents. Ben and Arlene Bennett refused to accept that Beau was gay. They believed Ethan was the devil and he'd seduced Beau. On more than one occasion, Ben had even asked their pastor if he'd exorcise Beau's demons. Needless to say, it made church awkward from time to time.

"Look," Ethan said, taking a deep breath. "We'll talk about this more. Not now, though. I honestly didn't mean to ruin our vacation."

Beau took a step closer. "You didn't ruin anything, E. You've managed to make me the happiest man on the planet, just being mine. And having a family with you... I know I've got a lot to deal with, and you're right, we need to talk more. We can even do that now. I just—"

Ethan put his finger over Beau's lips, silencing him. "We'll table this for now. I still want to have a family with you." He forced a smile. "I think we need to let that sink in first. Then..." Ethan leaned in and pressed his lips to Beau's. "We can work out the logistics later."

Beau nodded, resting his forehead against Ethan's.

"I love you, E. I hope you don't think I'm crazy."

"I love you, too," Ethan whispered, chuckling. "Despite the crazy."

It was only funny because everyone knew Beau was the level-headed one. If anyone was crazy, it was definitely Ethan.

"WE HAVE TO BE AT THE AIRPORT soon, Beau," Ethan announced. "Which means we have to hit the road to drive there. It took us two hours the first time."

Beau lifted his head from his pillow and glanced across the room, trying to locate the man who owned the voice. "What time is it?"

"Time for you to get out of bed." Ethan disappeared into the bathroom.

It was clear by the sound of things being moved around that Ethan was packing. Beau had offered to pack last night, but they'd decided to spend the evening in the hot tub. Although this time, Ethan had made Beau hold out for sex. Both then *and* when they'd crawled into bed.

"I'm not going to the airport," Beau announced, watching the bathroom door.

Ethan stuck his head out. "What?"

"Not until you come over here," Beau tacked on. "Since I know you're not gonna let me join the mile-high club, we're gonna have to settle this right here."

Ethan stepped into the bedroom, hands on his hips. "Settle what?"

Beau didn't move, didn't say anything more. He waited for Ethan to come over, which he did. The man was sometimes very predictable, especially when it came to having sex. Ethan often accused Beau of being insatiable, but they both knew it went both ways.

When Ethan approached the bed, Beau looked up into his eyes, trying to hold back his smile. He then moved the blanket off of him, letting Ethan see for himself just how hot the man made him. Beau reached down and grabbed his dick.

Ethan's eyes followed the movement, and sure enough, he was now fully focused on the way Beau was slowly stroking himself.

"I need your mouth," Beau told him. "Right now."

"Right now, huh?" Ethan met his gaze. "Or what? You're gonna die from not enough oral pleasure?"

"Don't joke about something like that," Beau deadpanned. "I hear it can happen. Don't let me be a victim."

Ethan laughed, which made Beau laugh, too. He couldn't help himself.

"Come on, E. Just a little … lick."

"And then what? I lick you once and you'll get dressed so we can go?"

Beau shook his head. "You lick me once, then I'll roll over and you can fuck me the way I know you want to."

Ethan's blue-gray eyes flared with heat.

Yep, Beau had definitely hit his mark.

Holding his breath, Beau watched as Ethan leaned over. Beau stopped stroking himself, holding his dick still so Ethan's wicked tongue could glide over the head.

"Oh, yeah," Beau hissed. "One more time."

Ethan licked him again.

"Please. Just one more time."

This time Ethan smiled as he licked him again and again and again.

"Oh, fuck…" Beau released his cock when Ethan sucked him fully into the furnace of his mouth.

Gripping the sheet beneath him, he watched his husband as he received one of the most amazing blow jobs he'd ever had.

"Oh, yeah… Fuck, E…" Beau didn't reach for Ethan, not wanting him to stop. It felt too good.

Of course, Ethan being Ethan, he quickly shed his clothes and joined Beau on the bed. He knelt between Beau's legs, sucking him while he forced Beau's legs up. When Beau finally caught on to what his intention was—because *come on*, the pleasure *was* making his brain a little foggy—he pulled his knees up into his chest and was rewarded when Ethan drifted lower, sucking Beau's balls into his mouth, laving him with his tongue.

"Oh, fuck … yeah … E… That's…"

A finger teased his asshole, and Beau dropped his head, closing his eyes as he was assaulted by exquisite sensations. He could so easily come like this, with Ethan's mouth on him, his fist jerking him, his finger fucking his ass. He could, but he wouldn't because he wanted Ethan to fuck him first.

"E… If you keep that up… Oh, fuck yessss…" He was close. Too close. "Fuck me, E. I'm begging you, baby. Slide your dick in my ass and fuck me like you need me."

And to prove how much he wanted it, Beau tossed the tube of lubrication he'd had hidden beneath his pillow.

"Turn over," Ethan instructed, snatching the lube and sitting up on his knees.

Beau managed to turn over, going up on his knees with Ethan still behind him. He waited, his body humming with anticipation.

"Not gonna be easy," Ethan warned.

"Don't want easy," Beau told him. "Want you. Now."

Ethan always said he wasn't going to be easy and it was mostly true. Expect for when he was preparing Beau. He was always thorough, always mindful that if he was too rough, he could hurt him. Not that Beau would've complained. He loved when Ethan lost control.

But right now, the waiting was torture. "Fuck. Me."

Beau felt the head of Ethan's cock nudging his asshole, and he relaxed as much as he could. When Ethan pushed forward, Beau thrust back, forcing Ethan inside in one spine-tingling rush.

"Oh, fuck…" Beau took a deep breath, the pain mixing with pleasure almost instantly.

Ethan's hands gripped Beau's hips, holding him still as he began to fuck him roughly, driving into him hard and fast. It was perfection and Beau held out, refusing to come until Ethan did. He was so damn close, biting his lower lip to keep from going over the edge.

"Tight… So tight, Beau. Goddamn… I'm gonna come in your ass… Can't … stop."

Beau held still, rocking back against Ethan as his husband slammed into him over and over again. And when Ethan jerked, his hands gripping Beau's hips tighter, he let himself go.

"Oh, yeah! Coming, E… Fuck, baby…"

Ethan fell on top of him, sweating and panting, but Beau didn't mind. He simply lay there, completely sated. Unfortunately, that didn't last long.

"Ouch!" Beau groaned when Ethan bit his shoulder. It was actually quite stimulating, but he knew Ethan had been trying to get his attention.

"We gotta go. You've got five minutes to shower and to pack."

Beau chuckled. "Baby, I packed last night, and I only need three minutes to shower."

BY THE TIME THEY GOT HOME, ETHAN was exhausted. They'd spent the majority of the day traveling—first driving back to Denver, then waiting a full three hours at the airport because their flight was delayed, the three-hour flight, then another half-hour drive from Austin to Coyote Ridge—and the time difference had only made it worse. Because they were both starving, they'd stopped by Mama's Diner for dinner on the way from the airport. Ethan didn't make a habit out of going out, but he was too damned tired to cook, so he'd given in to Beau's pleading.

After that, they stopped by his parents' house to let them know they were back. They didn't stay for long, but his mother made them promise to come by for Sunday dinner and fill them in on the trip. He promised that they would.

And now, they were home, once again in their own bed. Beau had the television on, but he continued to flip channels, meaning he hadn't found anything worthwhile to watch.

Not once since the other night had they talked any more about babies. Ethan continued to wait, hoping Beau would bring it up, but he didn't seem to have any intention of doing so. He now knew how Beau felt, because Ethan had been doing the same thing to him for months. But Ethan knew Beau wasn't doing it to get back at him.

Beau simply was torn on how to proceed.

Not that Ethan necessarily blamed him for his fears. Ethan would be the first to admit that sometimes irrational fears became so real it was impossible to let go of them. He'd spent his entire life hiding from everyone, including himself. While his family claimed they'd known he was gay long before he ever admitted it, they had never broached the subject, either.

And now, as Ethan lay in the dark, watching Beau in profile, he wondered how this would play out. One of these days, they would have to talk about it again. They would have to figure out a path to take, whatever that might be. Kids or no kids. Adoption or surrogate. With those came other decisions that had to be made. This parenting thing wouldn't be easy, but neither of them expected it to be. They'd both watched his brothers tackle the job on more than one occasion. Sometimes Ethan envied them; other times he didn't.

Nonetheless, he wanted to have a family with Beau.

So, while he continued to cherish every minute he had with this man, Ethan would continue to do research.

Along with options, they both had demons that they had to overcome.

Even two years later, Ethan was still seeing a therapist. His sessions weren't as frequent as they once had been, but even he had to accept that the therapy had helped. Significantly.

Maybe Beau would be interested in going. They could talk about his issues with his parents. God knew there were issues, and although Beau pretended that it didn't bother him, that his soul wasn't shredded because the two people who were supposed to love him unconditionally had written him off, Ethan knew that it did.

But there was one thing Ethan knew without a doubt. They both had trepidations and they had fears, but they also had each other. And when the time came to start the process—Ethan prayed it would be soon—they would hold each other up, because that was what love did. It gave you the strength to do things you never thought possible. Beau had been Ethan's strength for so long. Ethan was ready to return the favor.

Beau glanced over, smiling in the darkness.

Ethan smiled back. "I love you."

That seemed to make Beau's smile brighter, which made Ethan's heart swell in his chest.

Yes. That was what he wanted.

To put that smile on Beau's face.

Every single day.

For the rest of their lives.

 Early Christmas Present

Trace Kogan and Marissa Trexler

from *Wait for Morning*

The day before Thanksgiving…

TRACE KOGAN TOOK HIS WIFE'S HAND, PULLING her into him as he stared blankly at the wall, trying to see what she saw.

"Which color do you like better?" Marissa asked.

"Is there a difference?"

Marissa pulled back and lightly swatted him on the chest. "Of course there's a difference. One is gray and one is blue-gray."

"Then I like … that one." He pointed at the wall where she'd painted two small sections, waving his hand to encompass both.

"Which one?"

He rolled his eyes dramatically, knowing it would make Marissa laugh.

"The one *you* like best," he admitted. Trace knew that she would go with the one she liked better anyway. Not to mention, it really didn't matter to him. Paint, flooring, cabinets … none of that mattered to him. Throughout the time Marissa had taken on the project of remodeling the warehouse where they lived, Trace had tried to stay out of the decision-making. As long as his bed was a king and his woman was in it with him, he couldn't care less about the rest of it.

"We're going with blue-gray."

"Perfect. Exactly the one I was talking about."

"You're impossible, you know that?"

"I do," he confirmed. "It's my mission in life."

"Please tell me that wasn't a *Mission Impossible* reference."

"Okay, that wasn't a *Mission Impossible* reference," he echoed, grinning.

When Marissa headed for the kitchen, Trace diligently followed.

"What time is dinner tomorrow?" he asked, going right for the coffeepot. He was doing his best not to stare at her ass in those jeans. The woman made him so damn hard just by breathing, so when she wore stuff like that, his dick was in constant opposition with his zipper. Not a comfortable thing.

"Your mother said everyone needs to be there at six. And remember, she said everyone must be on their best behavior."

"Easier said than done," he grumbled.

"Oh, come on. This isn't the first time we've had Thanksgiving dinner at Max's house. No one ended up in the hospital the last time…"

Sometimes it was still hard to believe that Trace's sister had married Maximillian Adorite. However, Courtney was officially a mob boss's wife.

Trace thought back to the first Thanksgiving dinner they'd had at his brother-in-law's house. Admittedly, it hadn't been terrible, but merging the families wasn't a simple task considering the tension between the Kogans and the Adorites. Apparently, the feud had started years ago when Trace's father had dated Max's mother. Of course, that was long before Casper or Genevieve was old enough to know better and before Casper set out for the military, where he ultimately met Trace's mother and fell head-over-heels in love with her.

According to the tale, nothing had ever happened between Casper and the then-far-too-young Genevieve, but not everyone believed that. From what Trace had heard, Max's father, Samuel Adorite, had held a grudge for many, many years. Then again, the man had been unstable to start with, and he'd proven it by forcing Genevieve to marry him when she was merely a child. Now that Samuel was dead and their lives were inevitably joined together because Courtney had married Max, they were still trying to figure it all out.

"It'll be fine," Marissa stated reassuringly.

Trace nodded, draining the coffee that was left in the carafe before depositing it in the sink. He turned to face her, crossing his arms over his chest and sipping from his mug. Again, he found himself admiring the woman. From the top of her blond head all the way down to her cute little feet.

"Do you know how hard it is to keep my hands off you?"

Marissa's head snapped up, her ice-blue eyes locking with his. "You've actually been trying?"

Her smirk was enticing. "I've been trying," he confirmed.

"So how do you explain last night?"

Trace grinned. "I said I'm *trying*. Didn't say I was succeeding."

The truth was, Trace didn't want to keep his hands off her. Ever since the woman had told him she was ready to get pregnant, he'd turned into some sort of fiend. The fact that she was still on birth control didn't hinder his ability to screw her senseless, either. Because of his job, Trace was sometimes gone for days, even a couple of weeks at a time. Now that his brother Hunter was finally back from his overseas assignments, Trace was able to stay close to home most of the time.

Something he preferred.

After downing what was left of his coffee, he rinsed the cup and put it in the dishwasher. When Marissa was finished cutting up her fruit, he crowded her from behind, wrapping his arms around her. "I'm gonna miss you."

"You're gonna be home in time for Thanksgiving dinner tomorrow night, right?"

"I am."

"I'll miss you, too."

"Did you ever figure out what you wanted for Christmas?" he inquired. It was a question he'd been asking for several weeks now. It never got him anywhere, but he was certainly trying.

"I told you, it's not the same if I tell you what I want."

Leaning in, Trace pressed his lips to her neck. "Are you sure you want me to make that decision?"

"Of course I do."

"Well, then that makes it easy."

Marissa turned in his arms, smiling up at him. "Easy, huh?"

Trace nodded.

"Does that mean you already know what you're gonna get me?"

"Yep." He nibbled her earlobe. "And I'm gonna have to give it to you early."

His wife's confusion was etched on her pretty face, a wrinkle marring her flawless forehead. "Why's that?"

"You'll see. After dinner. Tomorrow night."

"A Christmas present a whole month early. I'm intrigued."

"You should be."

He tugged on the front of her sweater, pulling her closer so he could kiss her mouth.

"You're goin' to Courtney's tonight, right?"

"Yep. I offered to help them cook."

"And I'll meet you there for dinner tomorrow?"

"That's where I'll be."

He nodded, staring into her eyes. "I love you, baby."

Her smile widened and he saw the love shining in her eyes. "I love you, too."

"So…?" Courtney prompted.

Marissa pulled her feet up underneath her, watching her best friend closely. With Max out doing whatever it was that a mafia guy did, the turkey cooking for tomorrow, Marissa and Courtney had called out for Chinese, then eaten it on the heated back porch while they sipped wine and talked about nothing important.

They seemed to have drifted to another topic, and Marissa was once again not on the same page. "So *what?*"

"He didn't give you any other hints?"

Ahh. Trace's Christmas present. They were apparently back to that. She remembered the twinkle in his iridescent white-gray eyes, the way his perfect lips had curved into a wry smile. The man knew how to torment her when he wanted to.

"Not a one," Marissa admitted. "He told me he'd have to give it to me early."

"Did he say it like that?" Courtney inquired, a smirk on her face. "Did he specifically say 'give it to you'?"

Marissa shook her head, grinning. The woman had such a dirty mind.

It was almost uncanny how much the Kogans resembled one another. Like Trace and their other brothers, Courtney had thick, light brown hair and a strong jawline. They all had the same brilliant, nearly colorless eyes, too. Those eyes sometimes saw far more than they should.

Courtney giggled, probably enjoying the fact that Marissa blushed. "Fine. Don't answer that." She took a sip of wine. "What do you think it could be?"

Marissa shrugged as she pulled the blanket up on her lap. "There's no telling with Trace. He's always up to something."

Courtney seemed to mull that over. "Maybe it's a car?"

"I don't need a car."

"You aren't supposed to get what you *need* for Christmas. You get what the giver wants you to get."

Marissa considered that for a moment. "In that case, I'd have to assume it's sex."

Courtney chuckled. "You aren't getting that already?"

"Not as often as I'd like," she admitted. Trace had been gone a lot lately, leaving her sleeping alone. And when he was home, they were both busy. Work, family … it all got in the way of a meaningful, well-balanced relationship. The honeymoon was definitely over, but real life hadn't altered her intense desire for the man. Unfortunately, when the timing wasn't right, there wasn't a lot she could do about it.

"Well, you'd better call me the minute you know. I don't know if I'll be able to sleep until you tell me."

Marissa chuckled. "Oh, whatever. I'm pretty sure your husband takes good care of you. You probably pass out every night with a stupid grin on your face." Considering the way Courtney's mob boss husband couldn't seem to keep his hands off her, Marissa figured they were going at it every chance they could get.

"I'll say," Courtney grinned mischievously. "Max does know how to take care of his woman."

"You're bad."

"Funny." Courtney chuckled. "That's what Max says."

Marissa leaned back on the couch and relaxed. She missed Trace already, and she knew he would be back tomorrow. The short job he'd been assigned would only take him away overnight. She knew the only reason he'd taken an assignment that overlapped with Thanksgiving was because he'd asked to stay close to home for the next month. Marissa was looking forward to having him to herself for a while.

"Okay, girly, you're far too quiet. You need more wine."

"I'm game if you are."

Courtney cocked one dark eyebrow. "I'm always game. Wine is better than water." She grinned. "Speaking of wine. How do you think dinner will go tomorrow night?"

Marissa knew that Courtney was referring to the fact that the festivities were being held at Courtney's house. The one she shared with her mobster husband and the various minions the Adorites employed. It wasn't a secret that there was some tension between the Kogans and the Adorites. Not so much now that Courtney's father-in-law was no longer on this earth. The man had apparently had it out for Courtney's dad because of some fictional relationship he'd perceived to be going on between Max's mother and Casper a million years ago.

"I'm sure it'll be fine," Marissa consoled.

"You're right. Everyone loves Max."

"It's a good sign that we survived it two years in a row." Although Marissa hadn't been in attendance the first year, she had heard that the two families had been able to keep the peace. "But I'm not sure I'd go so far as to say that everyone loves Max. I don't think Hunter and Conner are all that fond of him."

"That's because they're too overprotective."

Marissa understood that all too well. She had a bunch of overprotective brothers as well.

"You're right," Marissa said with a chuckle. "I'm sure they *like* him. A little."

"Maybe I should order more wine. Like, six or seven bottles. Just to make sure everyone gets along well."

"It'll be fine." Although Marissa had married Courtney's brother a year and a half ago, they'd spent nearly every Thanksgiving and Christmas together since they were in diapers. After all, they had grown up together because of how close their families were. Since their fathers owned Sniper 1 Security, they were pretty much one big happy family.

"Of course, there is the little issue with…" Courtney pursed her lips as she stared at Marissa.

It took a second for her to realize what her friend was referring to. Or rather, who. "Dani?"

Courtney nodded.

"I'm sure Hunter is over her by now," Marissa stated, not sure whether that was the truth or not.

"I don't know about that. He's still pretty angry."

Not that Marissa blamed the guy. Courtney's brother had fallen in love with a woman who had left him at the altar and disappeared right after. Of course, Max, being Max, had insisted that it was time for her to come home where her family was. Turned out—which was possibly the most shocking thing of all—Danielle Davidson was Max's cousin.

Small world.

"Well, regardless, I'm looking forward to watching it all play out," Courtney noted.

"I'm sure Max will be on his best behavior. And Hunter, too."

"Is it bad that I'm worried more about everyone else?"

"Just think," Marissa told her, "if they want to make it to Christmas, they'll have to survive this. I'm sure everyone will be smiling."

Worst case, they'd all be *pretending* to smile.

CHAPTER 2

Trace made it back to Dallas just in time to grab a shower in one of the guest bedrooms at his sister's house. His parents were already there, and his brothers, as well as the Trexlers, were starting to arrive. From what he could tell, everyone had agreed to let bygones be bygones for the time being. Dinner would be served in half an hour, and he was anxious to see his wife. The overnight job had been one of those textbook personal security details. Some big-shot senator had needed some extra eyes on him during a speech he was giving.

Because it was a six-hour drive, Trace had stayed overnight and hopped on his motorcycle first thing this morning. He easily could've taken the company jet, but Trace happened to prefer the bike. He didn't get on the open road often, so when the opportunity presented itself, he couldn't refuse. He'd agreed to meet his brother Conner and drive the final two hours together. Although Trace had enjoyed every second of it, it'd been a long day already.

And it was only beginning.

A knock sounded on the bathroom door.

"Almost done," he called out, not sure who would be upstairs.

Turning off the water, Trace grabbed a towel and pulled back the shower curtain.

He came face-to-face with the sexiest woman on the planet.

"Courtney told me you were up here," she said sweetly. "Couldn't even kiss me hello?"

Trace noticed the teasing smirk on her lips. "I was washing off the dirt and grime so I could kiss you appropriately. Is that why you're in here? To kiss me hello?" he asked, wiping the water from his body, not even pretending to be modest. He liked the way his wife's eyes trailed over him.

"Thought I'd check on you. Make sure you weren't doing anything you shouldn't be doing."

"Like?"

He loved that his wife still blushed when she talked about sex. And yes, he knew what she was referring to. In recent weeks, whenever he returned from a job, no matter how short, Marissa was usually waiting for him. Naked.

Of course, she couldn't do that here, but her joining him in the bathroom was probably a sign that she was as eager as he was at the moment.

After drying off completely, Trace dropped the towel and crowded her between his body and the counter. He planted his hands on the sink, on each side of her hips, then kissed her on the nose.

"Do you know how hot it makes me when you watch me like that?"

Marissa grinned. "You say that about everything that I do."

"And it's true. Everything you do makes me hot."

"You should get dressed."

"What if I'd rather get you undressed?"

"Then I'm sure someone would come up here and find us sooner or later."

"And that's a problem, why?" Trace leaned in and kissed her lips, cupping her face gently. He tipped her head to the side before sliding his tongue into her mouth. What he wouldn't give to shove her jeans down to her ankles, to turn her around and slide into the warmth of her body. Damn it. Thinking about it wasn't helping his current state.

Marissa moaned softly, but she also pushed against his chest, giggling when he pulled back. "Someone's gonna find us in here."

"Ask me if I care."

"You might not, but I do. Maybe after dinner."

Trace's eyes widened, his interest piqued. "Yeah? In here?"

Her eyelashes lowered, her cheeks turning a pretty shade of pink. "If you're good."

"Darlin', I'm always good. But I'll be exceptionally good if you're offerin' what I think you're offerin'."

"When are you gonna tell me what my Christmas present is?"

Trace took a step back, smiling down at this crazy woman. "Is that why you snuck in here? You thought I'd tell you what it is before tonight?"

She shrugged. "Maybe. You didn't give me a time."

"I think I said after dinner."

"I don't remember that." Her smile said her memory loss was convenient.

He leaned in and kissed her on the forehead. "I promise, you'll know before we leave here."

"Really?" Her excitement danced in her pretty blue eyes.

"Really. Now get. I need to get dressed, and if you keep watching me like that, my jeans aren't gonna fit right."

Her gaze trailed down to his erection and his body caught fire.

"Marissa…"

She lifted her eyes to his, a picture of innocence. "Hmm?"

He didn't have to say anything. She must've seen it in his eyes because she chuckled and then sauntered right back out of the bathroom.

If it weren't for the gift he was giving her, Trace would probably take a few minutes to relieve himself. Since he was a man on a mission, that wasn't an option.

Which meant he needed to get dressed.

And fast.

No doubt about it, Max and Courtney's house was one of the nicest Marissa had ever been in. Travertine floors, stylish décor in every single room, a kitchen to rival most high-end restaurants. It was incredible, and despite the fact that goons were walking around, guarding Courtney and Max, as well as Max's brothers and sisters, Marissa didn't mind spending time here.

She knew the same couldn't be said for her family or even most of Courtney's. But today they were all on their best behavior. The conversation was light, the laughter continuous, and the only person who seemed to be pouting was Hunter. Again, Marissa didn't necessarily blame him.

Now that dinner was out of the way—a phenomenal spread that had been prepared by Max himself—everyone was retreating to the living room or out on the back deck to sit by the fire someone had started in the outdoor fireplace. With the temperatures still relatively mild, being outside wasn't a hardship.

Surprisingly, no fights had broken out, which was a plus. However, all eyes had been on Genevieve and Elizabeth when the two women had remained in the dining room discussing the old days. She wondered how hard that was for them. Knowing that, at some point in Casper's life, he'd had a thing for Genevieve, Marissa was sure Elizabeth had found it odd.

Or maybe not. Considering Genevieve had been twelve or thirteen at the time, it really had been young love, nothing serious. Especially since Casper had been significantly older. Marissa had heard that was the reason Casper had gone into the military, leaving so that Genevieve could have time to grow up. Of course, he'd met Elizabeth during that time, and his life had moved forward while Genevieve had been stuck in her own personal hell.

Having lived a relatively sheltered life, Marissa couldn't imagine what it had been like for Genevieve. Married to a crazy bastard at thirteen after that same crazy bastard had blackmailed Genevieve's father for his permission. Yuck.

But it seemed the past was rightfully in the past, where it belonged, and everyone was getting along for the sake of Max and Courtney, who were definitely in love.

The truth was, Marissa never knew what might happen at a family meal. The Kogans and Trexlers were a passionate bunch. Bring the ornery and hot-tempered Adorites into the mix and watch out. Tempers could flare with the slightest provocation, but tonight had been better than expected.

Now that the evening was progressing, some people had gone upstairs to play pool in the elaborate game room, others still relaxing with a drink in hand. Again, she noticed that Hunter was standing in the far corner of the room, drinking a beer and looking incredibly uncomfortable. Of course, he always seemed to be uncomfortable these days. Ever since he'd come back from his last overseas assignment, that was. Marissa's brother-in-law wasn't the same man he'd been back when Dani had been in his life, that was for sure.

Marissa glanced around the room, seeking out her husband. She found him talking to Max's brother Victor as they headed toward the kitchen.

She kept her eye on Trace, willing him to look at her. He looked mouthwateringly sexy as always, wearing a pair of faded Levis that showcased his phenomenal ass and long legs. The shirt he wore was snug across his back, outlining the definitive V shape of his body. Maybe she should have snuck in a quickie in the bathroom a short time ago.

Perhaps she would have if it hadn't been for the fact that she wanted to know what her present was and she wanted to know now. She'd never been a patient child, wanting to open one gift early before Christmas, then after doing that, begging for another and another. Her parents had finally cut that ritual off early, refusing to argue with her. Being that she was the only girl, Marissa had often gotten her way growing up, so it only made sense that they'd nipped that in the bud before it had gone to her head.

But Trace had teased her with it, so he should have to follow through. Instead, it seemed the man was making her wait.

Of course, her husband endeared himself to Lilah, her parents' live-in housekeeper, and Walter, Max's live-in butler, offering to do the dishes for them while they delivered coffee to those who wanted it and continued to chat incessantly between them.

Marissa admired Trace, her love for him growing even more than she thought possible. It wasn't that he was the sexiest man in the room—although he certainly was—but he was one of the most generous, always looking to do something for someone else. It was sometimes hard to believe that she'd grown up with this man, and after crushing on him for years, she'd somehow been lucky enough to marry him.

She considered every minute with him a gift.

Even when he was obviously ignoring her.

Marissa kept her eyes on him, waiting him out. He would eventually look her way because he knew what she was waiting for.

Finally, after half an hour of ogling him from the barstool while making small talk with Conner's fifteen-year-old daughter, Shelby, Trace gave her the attention she craved.

"Can I talk to you for a minute?" Trace asked Marissa while giving his niece a knuckle bump.

"Of course."

Shelby was instantly off to talk to someone else while Marissa allowed Trace to lead her out of the room. She could hear the pool balls clanking upstairs, the gentle hum of conversation coming from the living room. He seemed uninterested in going either of those places, and Marissa's stomach flipped with excitement.

He was going to give her the present he'd promised.

She knew, no matter what it was, she was going to love it.

CHAPTER 3

Meanwhile, in another part of the house…

DANIELLE DAVIDSON COULDN'T BELIEVE SHE'D ALLOWED MAX to strong-arm her into coming to this stupid dinner. She should've told him to go to hell, but that would've been rude. Not that she was opposed to being just that, but when it came to Max, she tried to refrain. So, rather than turn on the one person who had been keeping an eye on her since she'd returned to the States, Dani had come up with a way to make this a win-win for her.

It also helped that she'd timed her arrival perfectly, avoiding the dreaded family dinner. Thankfully, it looked as though they'd already finished that portion of this evening's hellish activities.

Because Max had married Courtney, Dani had known there would be more than Adorites in attendance at this family get-together. More accurately, Courtney's brother Hunter would be in attendance, and by showing up, Dani would appease her cousin, then, by approaching Hunter, she could, in essence, kill two birds with one stone.

Admittedly, now that she was here in Max's house, it seemed some of the nagging determination she'd harbored recently was waning.

Chin up, she mentally ordered. She could do this. She *would* do this. And once she'd spilled the beans to Hunter, she could get back to this life she'd just recently returned to, without all the guilt she'd been carrying around with her.

Despite her little pep talk, Dani was tempted to turn around and run out the same way she'd come in. With all the critical eyes tracking her as she moved across the room, the simple thing to do would be to disappear.

Again.

But … if she did that, and caved to what would clearly be the easy way out, there would be no way to get her life back. It was bad enough that Samuel Adorite had been dead for a year now, and she had yet to stop hiding completely. As far as she was concerned, she'd been on the run for long enough; it was time to stop and face the music. The threat to her was no longer, now that the old bastard was dead.

Okay, so that wasn't entirely true. However, if the horrific secret they'd been keeping was buried with him, then yes, she was finally free.

Well, almost. She still had to confess her reasons for hightailing it out of Dodge four years ago, but once that was done, she would be in the clear and able to move on. And this Thanksgiving meal was the perfect place to show the world that she was no longer putting miles on her Manolos. She'd picked this particular event for a reason. Namely because there were so many people. Here, she could confront Hunter Kogan and not risk having him go postal on her. She hoped.

Then again, Dani didn't even know if Hunter would speak to her after what she'd done to him all those years ago. And she couldn't blame him if he didn't.

Now that she thought about it, they'd been in a setting much like this one.

Only, instead of a festive holiday dinner, it had been a wedding.

Hers.

And his.

Talk about coming full circle.

Since a wedding required vows, hers didn't quite qualify, because they'd never made it that far. Nope, that'd been the day she'd chickened out, running far and fast from the one and only man she'd ever loved.

It'd been easier than living a lie, or so she told herself.

"Dani?"

Turning at the sound of her name, Dani came face-to-face with Hunter's mother and father, Casper and Elizabeth Kogan. They were looking at her with wide-eyed wonder, as though she'd come back from the dead.

In a way, she kind of had.

"Mr. and Mrs. Kogan," she greeted politely, her voice trembling only slightly.

"We're so glad you could make it," Liz replied, but Dani could see it for the lie that it was.

They were more than likely trying to figure out why she was there. How she fit into this whole fiasco. They definitely weren't happy to see her, but she hadn't expected any less. She'd done the unthinkable, leaving the man she was supposed to marry—who happened to be their son—at the altar and not contacting him even one time since.

If only they knew who she really was, why she'd come into their lives in the first place … they certainly wouldn't be smiling at her now—fake or not.

"I'm glad I could, too," she lied.

Because Max had insisted—the man was probably unable to make a request—that she attend, Dani had known how things would turn out. And because of the guarantee that she would be face-to-face with the one man who probably never wanted to see her again, Dani had opted not to seek Hunter out earlier than now. This might've been the family's holiday celebration, but Dani was using it for her own agenda. As a way to see Hunter, to convince herself that what she thought had been the love to end all had only been a figment of her imagination. Plus, to free her conscience by admitting to him the truth. Or most of it anyway.

"It's good to see you," Dani told Liz and Casper, desperately wanting to get away from her once-future in-laws. After all, Casper was the head of Sniper 1 Security, and she didn't doubt that he could probably single-handedly take her out before she ever made it across the room to her intended target.

Not that he would.

Hopefully.

"You, too," Liz whispered, staring after her as Dani headed off to make her way around the perimeter of the room.

She scanned the crowd, noticing Hunter's brother Conner and Conner's daughter, Shelby, sitting together on one end of the oversized cream sofa, along with RT and Z on the opposite end. She took a moment to give the two men a cursory glance. Seeing them together brought back a memory of two different men and a very sexy night from so long ago. A night she would never forget for as long as she lived. It'd been the night she'd moved out of her comfort zone, trusted the man she'd fallen in love with, and experienced sensations she'd never even imagined possible.

A night that she would never have again.

Shaking off the thought, Dani took stock of the room. Others had started to move in, some seated on Max's furniture, several standing around, looking as uncomfortable to be there as Dani imagined them to be. These were two families who were on opposite sides of the law. Yet, somehow, they managed to coexist, or so it appeared, despite what Samuel Adorite had been up to all those years ago.

Dani caught sight of Courtney and Max, walking into the kitchen, hand in hand.

As good as it would've been to see some of her old friends again— if they would even talk to her—Dani hadn't come here for that. She wasn't looking for friends from her past. She was looking for one man in particular.

As though magnetized, her gaze swung to the far corner of the room, closest to the floor-to-ceiling windows near the back entrance.

And there he was.

Hunter Kogan.

Her heart did a strange little jump kick in her chest, but she ignored it.

God, he looked good.

Six foot one inches of prime alpha male sporting dark jeans that showcased his impressive ass and a crisp white shirt that accentuated his broad shoulders and wide back. As though he sensed her looking his way, Hunter turned. She could practically see his white-gray eyes glowing from where she stood. His light brown hair was a little longer than before, shaggier, his face a little more weathered, but he was just as ruggedly handsome as he'd always been.

Without stopping to chat with anyone else, Dani snaked her way through the people, glancing toward the kitchen briefly to ensure Max wasn't watching her. So far, so good. He was the last person she wanted to run into at the moment, but only because their relation was supposed to be a secret. Only she knew that it was just another lie in a long list of them that'd been put in place over the years. Max might've believed that Dani was his first cousin, but she knew the truth.

However, she was only willing to divulge so much information.

Which she would do. Tonight.

But she needed it to be on her terms.

HUNTER KOGAN DIDN'T NEED TO BE DAMN good at his job to know that the proverbial shit was about to hit the fan. He'd felt the prickling at the back of his neck for several minutes now, and though he'd scanned the room, searching for a threat, he'd already suspected what he would find.

And sure as shit, the threat was real, only this one was a woman—oftentimes far more dangerous than any top-secret mission his family's security firm could send him on.

This particular woman decidedly so.

His cell phone buzzed in his pocket and he pulled it out.

Principal has arrived at the party. She had no issues walking right in.

The final confirmation of what he'd suspected. Danielle Davidson at Max Adorite's home. An invited guest, apparently.

Rather than respond to the agent he'd been using to follow Dani around since she'd miraculously reappeared in town several months ago, Hunter tucked his phone into his pocket. Although sneaking out the back door was ideal, he managed to remain motionless, pretending not to be affected by the determined chick who was making her way across the room toward him.

Truth time. He knew it. She knew it.

He hated it. Based on the extreme look of discomfort on her face, she did, too.

Good. At least they were on the same page.

Fuck.

But why did it have to be here? Now?

Even from across the room, he recognized that resolute gleam in her golden eyes. She was on a mission, and those sexy legs were carrying her right to her intended target.

Maybe he should run.

Though it was long overdue, Hunter suddenly didn't want to talk to her, didn't want her to share with him the reason she'd fucked his world beyond repair years ago. He didn't want to know the truth. Her version, that was. He didn't want to know anything at all. He simply wanted to continue pretending to be blissfully ignorant, drinking his Corona, talking to his brother, and acting as though he didn't know the sinfully beautiful woman whose attention seemed to be focused on him. The same sinfully beautiful woman who'd left him at the altar five goddamn years ago.

The same one who had crushed his heart into fucking dust.

Danielle Davidson. Max Adorite's fucking cousin.

Yeah. She thought no one knew that little secret, but he certainly did.

"You've got incoming, bro," Conner muttered in warning before turning away from Hunter and leaving him standing there, completely vulnerable.

Asshole.

"Hunter."

The sound of his name on her lips was very much as he remembered. For fuck's sake, he still heard that raspy tenor in his dreams.

Not by choice.

Opting for polite—this was his sister's home, after all—Hunter met her gaze. "Danielle," he replied, tipping his beer bottle to his lips as he peered down at her. "Surprised to see you here."

"No, you're not," she countered hotly, her eyes belying her frustrated tone.

What he saw in those glittering gold eyes wasn't animosity. If he didn't know better, Hunter would be inclined to believe she actually felt bad for what she'd done to him, leaving without ever looking back.

Too bad he did know better, and he wasn't falling for it again.

Setting his empty beer bottle on the tray of a passing waiter—a *waiter*, for chrissakes, at a family dinner—Hunter grabbed Dani's arm, pulling her deeper into the corner. Even in those four-inch heels, he towered over her and he needed that. Anything to give him the advantage. Bending down, he went nose to nose with her, refusing to inhale, not wanting to be reminded of how fucking good she used to smell.

"What the fuck are you doing here?"

Her eyes widened, but she didn't flinch. "We need to talk."

Hunter was tempted to laugh in her face, but he managed to refrain. "Talk? You're a few years too late for that, aren't ya, sweetheart?"

Dani frowned, and Hunter could feel that vise on his heart tighten.

She was the very reason he'd spent the last few months out of the country again, working any assignment that would keep him as far from here as possible. Here being anywhere she was. He'd known she was coming back, known she was planning to seek him out, and no matter how hard he tried, he hadn't been able to avoid the inevitable. Hence, he'd assigned Kye Sterling to keep an eye on her for the past few months. Hunter had been apprised of her whereabouts for three very long, very painful months.

And here she was, ready to chat.

He wasn't going to be her goddamn whipping boy this go-round. He didn't give a shit about her trying to get out from under the weight of her conscience, either. And damn it all to hell, seeing her now, the anger was boiling in his veins. But along with that, there was something else.

Longing.

He felt like his heart had been pierced with an arrow. And it damn sure hadn't come from fucking cupid.

Stupid fucking bastard.

Yep, he was, and arguing with that stupid-ass voice in his head wasn't going to make a damn bit of difference.

"Whatever you have to say," he began, keeping his tone hard, "I don't wanna hear it."

"I think you do," she said simply.

Hunter stood to his full height, glaring down at her as he studied her face. "Why here? Don't you know this is supposed to be a family event, Danielle?" A family she'd decided she didn't want to be part of. "Don't you have even a little respect for *my* family?"

Another frown creased her beautiful face, and he almost felt a measure of remorse. Almost.

"You're not an easy man to track down," she replied.

No, probably not. But that'd been on purpose. He didn't bother telling her as much; he assumed she already knew he'd spent the last couple of months avoiding this exact scenario.

"Get on with it," he urged. "But first, I need another beer."

Without worrying about social etiquette, Hunter walked away from Dani, making a beeline for the bar. No one other than Max Adorite would have a fucking bar in his house, complete with hired help to man it. After placing his order, Hunter stood there, resting his forearms on the sleek wooden top while he tried to calm his nerves. Part of him wished he'd simply invited Kye to be here with him tonight. It would've made this a little less painful.

Or maybe not.

After nodding to the bartender when he delivered his Corona, Hunter downed half of the beer, wondering just how many of them he'd need to make it through this conversation without wanting to put his fist through the wall.

A glance behind the bar and Hunter figured there wasn't enough liquor in the place to make this easy on him.

No matter how much he wished there was.

Casting a glance at Dani over his shoulder, he noticed she seemed deflated. As though she was lacking the bravado she'd had moments ago.

"What is it?" he questioned roughly, turning to face her.

"You know what?" Dani shook her head. "Never mind. This was a bad idea. A really bad idea. No matter what I say, you're still going to hate me."

He considered probing her for details, but she was right. He didn't need to hear them. It wouldn't change a thing, so he admitted as much. "You're right. Nothing you can do or say will ever change the way I feel about you. Nothing."

Her eyes widened, and this time Dani flinched, as though the heat of his words had been a physical blow. As with her excuses, he didn't care how he affected her. She'd earned his anger, his disdain, his ... hatred.

Dani's mouth opened but then closed quickly. Hunter forced himself to stay rooted where he was, glaring back at her, daring her to say something.

With a nearly imperceptible nod, Dani squared her shoulders, spun around on her heel, and left the same way she'd come.

Hunter should've been relieved, only he wasn't. However, he had to remind himself that Danielle Davidson was his past, and he damn sure didn't have room for her in his future.

No matter how much ... he really didn't hate her.

Trace knew he should probably take his wife home, but he couldn't resist the temptation before him. The thought of sneaking off with Marissa and finishing what she'd started in the bathroom earlier was too great. He wouldn't make it home before he stripped her and buried himself in her heat, so it only made sense to take her somewhere they could get a few minutes of privacy.

"Where are we going?" she asked.

"Garage."

"My present's in the garage?" She didn't sound happy about that.

"Not exactly," he told her, grinning to himself. "But it will be."

Trace found the small storage closet he'd been going for. He knew Max's home like his own because he always made a point to check things out and he'd gotten familiar with the garage/car showroom the first time he'd been invited to his sister's house. He also knew the storage closet in the garage held very little in it, plus, like the rest of the garage, the damn thing was air-conditioned, which meant it would be relatively comfortable.

Not that it would be for long. Once he got his hands on this woman, he was going to make her go up in flames. Or that was his intention anyway.

"Trace…?"

"Trust me."

Marissa harrumphed, making him chuckle.

He opened the closet door, then tugged her inside, pulling the door closed behind him. There was no lock, but the risk of someone finding them in there was one he was willing to take. Trace doubted anyone would come looking for them for a good twenty minutes or so.

Which meant he had to work fast.

Marissa peered around as though searching for something. Trace took her wrists in his hands and turned her to face him, pulling her close. He didn't waste words, pressing his mouth to hers.

"Is this my present?" she whispered against his mouth. "If so, I'm thinking you might have to brush up on your choices. What could possibly be in here that I'd want for Christmas?"

"Me," he mumbled, letting his hand drift beneath her sweater, sliding higher until he found the warm weight of her breast. He hefted it gently, raking his thumb over her nipple.

"Ahh. Well, in that case…" Marissa leaned into him, smiling.

"It's a little more than this," he told her, pulling back to look into her eyes.

Marissa was staring up at him, so much love reflecting back it made his heart twist in his chest. It didn't seem to matter that he'd snuck her into the closet of her best friend's garage or that he was currently groping her; the woman still looked at him as though he were the only man on the planet. He loved that shit.

"More than this?" She giggled. "What in the world are you up to, Trace Kogan?"

He grinned, giving her his best seductive smirk.

She didn't say anything.

Trace took a deep breath. He'd been thinking about this nonstop for a couple of months now. Now that their lives had settled down, he was ready for the next phase. So, he decided to tell her so.

"I want to have a baby with you, Marissa."

Her eyes widened and her lips curved up in a sweet smile. "Well, this is a good start."

"I'm serious," he explained. "I'm ready, Marissa. Ready to start a family with you."

He knew she'd been ready for some time, and they'd talked about it. They were both in agreement that they wanted kids—several, in fact—but they'd been holding out, wanting to make sure it was the right time. As far as Trace was concerned, there was no better time than right now.

"Me, too," she replied softly. "I want that more than anything."

He cupped her cheek. "Then no more birth control?"

She nodded, giggling. "Done. Well, not technically done, but tomorrow … I won't take any more."

Trace slanted his mouth over hers, pulling her closer, tightening his hand around her breast, needing to feel more of her against him. He was hard and aching for this woman. Every single thing she did turned him on. And the thought of her pregnant with his child… Damn.

"So this is my gift?" she questioned, a sweet smile on her face.

"It's one that keeps on giving," he told her, an answering grin on his face. "After all, I'm gonna have to work for it. But I'm up to the task."

"So endless sex until I get pregnant?"

"That's how it works, right?"

Marissa chuckled. "You're a mess, you know that?"

"I'm *your* mess."

"True."

Her fingers curled into the waistband of his jeans, and he felt her fingertips slide over the head of his cock. Trace sucked in air, then fastened his mouth to hers once more. He took all that she was willing to give and gave back just as generously.

Within minutes, they were practically clawing at one another, clothes hanging off them as Trace turned her so that her back was to the wall, her breasts crushed to his chest. Knowing they were short on time, the foreplay was limited, but she didn't seem to mind any more than he did. Drugged by her kisses, he pushed inside her, feeling the warmth of her body clasp him.

"Oh, yeah," he groaned. "Your pussy feels so damn good."

Marissa's hands slid down to his ass, her fingernails digging into his flesh as she pulled him closer.

Trace didn't need to be told twice. He began rocking into her, pushing as deep as possible, retreating slowly. His tempo increased as he kissed her, his tongue in tune with the rhythm of his hips.

"More." Marissa's body quivered around him as he continued to drive into her, trying not to make a sound, not wanting to bring someone running out to see what they were doing. "Right there … Trace … right there."

He drove into her, giving her what she asked for, allowing her body to drag the pleasure from him. It didn't take long before he was riding the fine line between heaven and hell, desperate to send her over.

When she cried out his name, her body gripping him like a vice, Trace let go, following her over. He came for what felt like an eternity, his breath lodged in his throat. When his sanity returned, Trace helped his wife right her clothes and did the same with his own before leading her back into the house. She snuck into the bathroom while he darted up the stairs to the game room. He was all for a quickie but definitely didn't want to take on Marissa's brothers. They were still a protective lot.

And as he settled in with the others, he found himself already thinking about the next time he could have her.

MARISSA COULDN'T HELP HERSELF. AFTER SHE CLEANED up, she went in search of her best friend. She knew Courtney was waiting to find out what her gift was, and Marissa was more than excited to tell her. She found Courtney in the living room, sitting beside Max, listening to Casper and Bryce tell stories of their early days at Sniper 1 Security. Ashlynn, one of Max's sisters, as well as Ashlynn's husbands, Jase and Leyton, were also there, hanging on every word. Marissa had heard all the stories before, more than once, in fact, as had Courtney, so she didn't feel bad stealing her away.

"Did he buy you a car?" Courtney whispered as Marissa tugged her into the kitchen. "I saw him take you to the garage."

Marissa chuckled, peering around to make sure no one was watching. "Not a car."

"Well? Don't keep me hanging."

Marissa's heart swelled. "He wants to have a baby."

"And he's giving you one for Christmas?" Courtney clapped her hands together.

"Well, probably not for Christmas. But we are gonna start trying." And if they did get pregnant by Christmas... Her heart swelled in her chest, filling with hope.

"So no more birth control?"

"No more," Marissa confirmed.

Courtney threw her arms around Marissa, hugging her tightly. Marissa hugged her best friend back, feeling the excitement welling in her belly.

A baby.

Part of her couldn't believe that this was really happening. Sure, she and Trace had talked about children, but neither of them had been sold on the idea of starting a family just yet. At twenty-six, Marissa was still a little worried that she wouldn't be a good mom. She was young and her marriage was in its early stages. Admittedly, it felt like the right time to her now, though.

"I'm so happy for you. I knew y'all would decide to have a family soon."

Marissa nodded. "We've talked about it. We agreed we would know when the time was right."

"And this is what you want?" Courtney's concern was reflected in her eyes.

"It is. Very much so."

"Well, then, what the hell are you doing hanging out here? Shouldn't you be at home, naked?"

Marissa giggled, feeling like a teenager again. "I'm sure that's coming."

"You mean you. *You're* the one who'll be coming."

"Oh, hush."

"What's goin' on in here, ladies?"

Marissa spun around to see her brother standing beside his husband, their eyes scanning the room. RT and Z were both watching them intently, likely trying to figure out what they were plotting. She didn't want them to think too hard on it because the pair of them were probably going to figure it out if they did. Marissa knew she couldn't hide the excitement on her face.

"The real question is, what are *y'all* doin' in here?" Courtney asked, clearly changing the subject.

"Dessert," Z stated, as though that made perfect sense. Of course, it kind of did. This was the kitchen; it was Thanksgiving.

"Is everyone ready?" Marissa inquired, turning toward the pies on the counter.

"I'm not sure about everyone else, but I am," Z stated. "That's all that matters."

Marissa chuckled. The guy did not shy away from food. It was a wonder he managed to keep his physique with the way he ate. As it was, Zachariah Tavoularis didn't have an ounce of fat on him. "If you say so."

Courtney offered a quick wink before disappearing and leaving Marissa to help dish out pie with her brother and brother-in-law. She knew they were watching her, knew they saw the smile permanently imprinted on her face.

As much as she enjoyed spending time with her family, Marissa was eager to get home. She wanted to get Trace alone for a little while. After all, she fully intended to hold him to his gift. It didn't take much for him to seduce her on any given day, but now…

God. A baby.

Marissa wasn't sure she'd be able to keep from jumping him every chance she got. Smiling to herself, she wondered if he even knew what he'd gotten himself into.

CHAPTER
5

Thursday, December 1st

"Trace?" Marissa called out from the other room.

"What, baby?" he called back from his office, peering up at the door when he heard her footsteps coming toward him.

"What is this?" She held up the package to show him. "It was just delivered."

"Ah. Perfect timing." He tried to pretend to be serious, but it was a hell of a lot harder than it looked, considering this item had come. "I've been waiting for that thing to get here."

"That thing?" She looked far too curious for her own good.

"Just a little Christmas present."

Marissa frowned. "I thought you already gave me my present."

"This one's for *us*," he explained. "But I need to do a few things to it first, then I'll show you."

She stared at him blankly, making him chuckle.

"Don't worry, you'll love it. I promise. And it's nothing fancy, so don't freak out."

"No more presents, Trace. You already have to deliver on the one you promised," she said, the twinkle in her eye softening her demanding tone.

"Oh, I'll deliver, all right," he assured her.

Marissa studied the box once more before setting it on the desk and then turning to go. He wanted to stop her and explain—he knew she wasn't big on the idea of being kept in the dark—but he really did need to do something first.

When she left the room, Trace opened the top drawer of his desk and pulled out the small, folded sheets of paper he'd put there a couple of days ago, then got to work opening the box. He pulled out the item inside and laid it flat on the desk.

It really wasn't anything fancy, but it was nice, and they could use it again next year and the year after. Not only for what he had in mind. It was a simple Advent calendar, a wooden box with twenty-five little doors, each with a small holiday picture carved on the front. Reindeer, trees, stockings, hearts, snowflakes. Cute but not over the top. After all, it wasn't the box that was the most important part of this gift.

Ten minutes later, with everything in place, Trace carried the box to the kitchen, where he found Marissa sitting on a barstool playing on her phone.

Her eyes widened when she looked up at him.

"It's nothin' fancy," he told her, placing the box on the bar in front of her.

"Is that an Advent calendar?" she questioned, her eyes grazing the outside.

Okay, good, so she knew what it was. When he'd gone looking online for one, he'd found they had a million different types. He wanted a simple one that had small boxes for the countdown so that he could place the sheets of paper in each little box.

"It is." He pointed at the number twenty-five. "And this is the one you open today."

"So, every day I open one of these doors and get a surprise as we count down to Christmas?" Her eyes were wide, hopeful. Like a kid on Christmas.

Trace pressed up against her, sliding his hand up to the nape of her neck. "Somethin' like that."

He watched as she pulled open the tiny wooden door marked with twenty-five. When she pulled out the sheet of paper, he clamped his lips shut, waiting patiently.

MARISSA KNEW EXACTLY WHAT AN ADVENT CALENDAR was. Her mother had insisted on the family having one when she was a kid. Granted, she seriously doubted that her dirty-minded husband had slipped pieces of candy or small trinkets inside each one of those boxes the way her mother had. He was far too devious for that.

Pulling open the small door, she noticed a tiny slip of paper inside, folded several times. Even without opening it, Marissa was pretty sure she already knew what was on it. No way was it a poem or a Christmas carol.

Taking the paper out, she looked from it to her husband, then back again.

She slowly unfolded it, continuing to watch her husband's face as she did, before glancing down at the paper. There, scrawled in Trace's very own chicken-scratch handwriting were the words: *Sex on the couch.*

"It's nice to see you started out tame," she said on a laugh. "I assume these get more devious as we go along?"

Glancing over her shoulder, she saw the grin on Trace's face. Yep. She'd thought so.

"So, just to confirm," she said calmly, peering down at the paper once more, pretending to study it, "every day I'm going to open one of these little doors to find out what sexual position we're gonna try for that day?"

Trace leaned in, his mouth warm on her neck as he kissed her gently. "That's the idea."

"You're a sneaky man, Trace Kogan."

Knowing Trace, sex on the couch was the tamest of them all. He was far more adventurous when it came to sex than she was. Not that Marissa minded, and she had to admit, this was a rather interesting game that he wanted to play. It went right along with them wanting to have a baby.

She only hoped she could survive twenty-five days of this.

CHAPTER 6

Sunday, December 4ᵗʰ

IT WAS INEVITABLE.

From the minute she had decided on a paint color, Trace had known he would be roped into doing the work. Granted, Marissa was willing to help, but he would've preferred to sit this one out and watch her. After all, she was sporting those cute overalls that had his dick doing a happy dance.

"Brush or roller?" she asked, squatting down to open the paint can.

He preferred neither. "Whichever. Doesn't matter."

Trace noticed Marissa shaking her head. She'd probably expected that answer. When she stood up and handed him the roller, he realized he wasn't getting out of this one.

"I hope this is the last room you're gonna paint," he grumbled, dipping the roller in the paint pan.

"No promises," she said sweetly.

Of course not.

They worked in silence for a few minutes, but then Marissa stopped. He could see she was observing him. Yeah, he was probably going slower than was necessary, but he enjoyed giving her crap for this sort of thing. It was a husband's duty to do so.

"I've got an idea," Marissa noted.

Trace paused, glancing over at her. "Yeah?"

"Since today's sex assignment is standing up—not very adventurous, by the way." She rolled her eyes. "I'm thinking I can add a little something."

That certainly got his attention. And she was right, standing up wasn't very adventurous, but he was trying to take it slow with her. Marissa was all for sex, but in all fairness, he didn't want to push her too far.

"What'd you have in mind?" he asked.

"For every wall you paint, I'll take off an article of clothing."

He looked her over from head to toe. She wasn't wearing socks or shoes, so that was a plus. That left a T-shirt, the overalls, and probably a bra and panties. He glanced at the four walls.

"That's good incentive," he admitted.

Damn good incentive.

MARISSA KNEW THE SECOND SHE MENTIONED STRIP painting that her husband would be on board. However, she hadn't realized how quickly he would work.

"One wall down," he announced, grinning from ear to ear. "Do I get to pick which article of clothing comes off?"

She smiled to herself. "I guess."

"Lose the shirt."

That was an interesting choice. However, a deal was a deal, so Marissa easily slipped her T-shirt off, leaving the overalls intact. She was mostly covered, so she went back to work.

Twenty minutes later, Trace was announcing he was finished with another wall. Marissa set her paintbrush down and turned to inspect his work. Sure enough, he'd knocked out another one in record time.

"Lose the bra, Marissa."

Of course.

Feeling her cheeks heat, Marissa unclasped her bra, then slipped it down her shoulders, tossing it to the floor with her shirt. There was a definite draft.

"Fuck," Trace groaned, his eyes locked on her.

She could see the telltale bulge in his jeans, and for whatever reason, that made her feel good. Marissa liked that she could get him hot and bothered.

"Get back to work," she said sternly.

"Take the straps off your shoulders," Trace commanded. "Let them hang down."

That would leave her topless completely. She considered it for a moment. "Not until you're halfway done with that wall."

Not surprisingly, Trace went right back to work.

Ten minutes later, Marissa was painting topless, her overalls hanging down. It was weird, for sure, but she pretended not to notice.

It wasn't long before she was clad in only her panties, but it appeared the final wall wasn't going to get completed anytime in the near future. Trace had dropped the roller and had her backed up against the only unpainted wall, his mouth fused with hers, his fingers dipping into her panties.

Because she'd been doing this little striptease for the past hour, Marissa was as worked up as he was, eager for him to finish what she'd started.

When he stripped her panties from her body, she didn't complain. And when he lifted her off her feet, Marissa wrapped her legs around him and allowed him to impale her.

"Oh, yes…" This was one hell of a way to spend a Sunday afternoon.

She couldn't wait to see what was in store for tomorrow.

Tuesday, December 6ᵗʰ

TRACE GOT THE DISTINCT IMPRESSION THAT HIS pretty little wife was being sneaky. He didn't know that for certain, but it seemed as though she'd started sneaking peeks at the future calendar days. It made sense. Marissa wasn't good with surprises. He probably should've only put one slip of paper into the Advent calendar at a time so she couldn't look into the future.

But he had a plan to counteract her deviousness.

One that involved her getting naked. Right now.

"Marissa?" Trace stepped into the kitchen, starting a pot of coffee.

"Huh?" she asked when she came into the living room. Ever since they'd finished painting the room, she'd been working on getting it decorated. Pictures, lamps, furniture, rugs… It seemed to be a never-ending process.

"Can you come here for a minute?"

She set down a picture on the coffee table and came toward him. "What's up?"

Trace leaned against the counter, regarding her for a moment. "Have you been peeking at days on the calendar?"

Her cheeks instantly turned a pretty shade of pink, and she didn't answer. Which meant he'd busted her.

Trace sipped his coffee, knowing she would have an excuse any second now.

"You didn't say I *couldn't* look," she blurted defiantly.

Fair point. "But I didn't say you *could*, either."

"True."

"Come here." He set his coffee mug on the counter as she approached slowly.

"What are you gonna do?" Her eyes widened, but there was a glimmer of heat reflected there. If he didn't know better, he would've thought she'd been hoping for this.

"I'm suddenly interested in watching you decorate that room," he told her, taking her hand and leading her back toward the new formal living area. He picked up the picture as he went.

"What's the catch?" she asked.

"I'm thinking it would be a much more interesting project if"—he grinned—"you were naked."

Her eyebrow lifted and he could tell she wasn't completely opposed to the idea.

"Naked?"

"Yep." He set the picture down on the chair, then reached for her shirt.

Without waiting for permission, he lifted it over her head and tossed it to the couch.

"You seem to have this thing with me stripping for you," she muttered.

"If I recall, you're the one who wagered that the other day."

Marissa rolled her eyes.

Trace took a step back until his calves hit the edge of the chair. "Now, I'll just sit here and watch while you get rid of the rest of those pesky clothes, then finish what you were doing."

MARISSA TRIED TO PRETEND SHE WASN'T BOTHERED by the fact that her husband had ordered her to strip naked to hang pictures. If she thought painting while partially naked was weird…

Still, she did it because Trace probably doubted that she would. And yes, he'd busted her. She had been peeking at the days to see what was on his list. She knew he'd caught her when she'd opened the box yesterday to find out that instead of having sex in the shower, they were going down to the garage to do so. It had been interesting to say the least.

However, she should've come clean at that point. Since she hadn't…

Well, this was her punishment.

Then again, watching Trace while he was watching her move naked across the room… It was rather exciting. The way his eyes followed her made her feel sexy despite her modesty.

But when she realized he had freed his cock from his jeans, that was when things got really interesting. At first she pretended not to notice, sneaking sideways glances at him. That didn't last long when he began stroking himself. The man was delicious, and when he was doing that … she was riveted to the sight.

"Come here, baby," Trace ordered, his voice low, commanding.

Marissa moved toward him without thinking.

His hand continued to stroke his long, thick length even when he reached for her, tugging her down so that she was kneeling between his thighs.

"I wanna feel those sweet lips on my dick."

God, she loved when he talked like that. She had no idea why, either. It simply did something for her. Her body heated instantly.

Marissa allowed him to guide her head down, her mouth opening as she licked the wide, swollen head. Within seconds, she was completely immersed in giving her husband as much pleasure as he could take.

"I want to fuck you… Ah, God, baby… That feels so damn good."

She didn't stop, even when he tried to pull her away. Marissa knew what he was doing, but she wanted to make him come like this.

"Marissa … oh, fuck." His fingers tightened in her hair, sending electric shocks dancing down her spine. "Keep that up and I'm not gonna be able to stop."

That was exactly what she wanted.

And she'd always been the type to go after what she wanted.

8

Thursday, December 8th

"MARISSA!" TRACE HOLLERED WHEN HE CAME INTO the warehouse two days later. When Trace's best friend fell in love with Marissa's oldest brother, RT, Trace and Marissa decided to convert the entire place to one large living space. Both floors. So now, they lived on the first and second floors, which, in a place this size, made it difficult to find his wife when he was looking for her. "Where are you?"

Stepping out of the kitchen, wiping her hands on a towel, Marissa watched him, surprise and curiosity etched on her pretty face. "What're you doin' home so early? I thought you were gonna be working late today."

Trace grinned. "It's three thirty. I don't consider that early."

"Any time before six is early for you," she countered.

True. She had him there.

Shrugging out of his jacket, Trace watched his beautiful, sexy wife play the sweet, innocent woman. He knew she was trying to anticipate his next move. That was what she did.

"What were you doing?" he asked.

"Deciding what I want to make for dinner," she stated, her gaze still locked on him, a cautious gleam sparkling there.

"Did you come up with something?" He tossed his keys on the table.

"Not yet, no."

"Well, I've decided what *I* want for dinner," he told her as he shrugged out of his jacket.

"And that would be?"

Not wanting to leave her hanging, Trace tossed his jacket onto a chair and stalked her.

"You, baby. That's what I want for dinner."

Her smile was almost instant, making his entire body harden.

"How did I know you were gonna say that?" she teased.

He loved to see her smile, to hear her laugh. He was thankful that she did both often. She was a ray of sunshine in his otherwise dark world. Although he loved his job, Trace still spent most of his time protecting people from various dangers that were threatening them. He liked that he could come home to her, to ignore the ominous threats to other people for a little while.

Granted, the worst threat he'd ever faced had been the one to this very woman. A madman had thought she knew too much based on some information she'd obtained, and he'd stalked her for years, always finding her despite the fact her father had stashed her in numerous safe houses. Thankfully, that threat had been eliminated—by Trace's brother-in-law, in fact—so he no longer had to think about that horrific time.

Trace focused his attention on his wife, thinking about this moment only. Right here. Right now.

"I'm thinking you have on too many clothes," he mused, watching as she backed up to the bar.

"I'm thinking that you should've called to warn me you were coming home."

"Where's the fun in that?"

"Well, maybe I could've showered or something," she said, laughing when he pressed his body to hers.

"Showers are overrated."

Marissa's eyebrow curved up, clearly in disagreement. "Not when you've been scrubbing the refrigerator all day."

"All day?" He gave her a speculative look. "Our refrigerator wasn't dirty enough to warrant an all-day cleaning."

"Whatever."

Despite her argument, he could smell her sweet fragrance, one that was unique to her. It was probably her shampoo or perfume, but it was still something that made him think of this incredible woman.

"Come shower with me," he whispered, leaning down and brushing his lips over hers.

"Who's gonna finish cleaning the fridge?" she asked, leaning back and smiling up at him.

"I will," he told her.

"Really? Trace Kogan is going to clean the refrigerator? Right. Next, you'll agree to do it in the nude."

"Would you like that?" he taunted. "Because I will. You know I will."

Marissa giggled, then tried to escape him. Trace caught her up in his arms and easily flipped her over his shoulder before carrying her toward their bedroom. It had been nearly two weeks since he'd promised to give her a baby for Christmas, and he was dedicating as much time as possible to ensure that happened. There were a couple of days he'd missed, but that was only due to life getting in the way. Truthfully, the Advent calendar was making for some interesting evenings.

Of course, he'd managed to sneak in as many quickies as possible, but as far as Trace was concerned, he hadn't been inside this woman nearly enough lately. If he had his way, he would be inside her at least three times a day. Maybe four.

He hadn't told his wife this yet, but the time for them was now.

"Trace Kogan, you better put me down," Marissa insisted, pounding his back with her fist.

He laughed, ignoring her protest as he walked through their bedroom and straight to the bathroom. He flipped on the shower before putting her down beneath the spray.

Thank God for instant hot water.

"What are you doing?" she squealed, brushing her hair back from her face.

Damn, she looked good wet.

"Kissing you," he said, right before he did just that.

Not surprisingly, Marissa gave up the fight, allowing the water to run over both of their fully dressed forms. He backed her against the tile, licking his way into her mouth, the familiar taste of her going to his head like his favorite scotch.

This right here... This was what he lived for. Coming home to her every single day.

MARISSA SHOULD'VE EXPECTED TRACE'S BARBARIC ADVANCES. IT certainly wasn't the first time he'd tossed her over his shoulder like a bag of flour. Nor was it the first time she'd seen that gleam in his eye.

Then again, she'd had to hold out on him for several days there at the beginning, since after stopping her birth control pills, she'd gotten her period and had to deal with that. Of course, Trace had more than made up for that already. If she were lucky, that was the only time they'd have to worry about it for the next nine months or so. God, she hoped that was the case and not because of the inconvenient timing of her monthly cycle but because she was hoping to get pregnant.

It would've been so easy to insist that she was busy, argue with him until he stopped pursuing her, but ... well, truth was, she didn't want to. Seriously. What sane woman would choose cleaning the refrigerator over taking a shower with the sexiest man on the planet? She was no dummy.

And not only because they were trying to have a baby, but also because she knew that this was one of those rare, special moments between the two of them.

After all she'd endured in the last few years, Marissa certainly knew that every single minute was a blessing. Having lived her life on the run for so many years, hiding from a madman who had set his sights on her, Marissa had come to cherish the simple things.

Yes, she'd gotten a little sappy since she'd said *I do*. And yes, Marissa spent the majority of her days smiling at all the memories they'd made together in the past couple of years. All in all, she knew she was blessed.

Of course, the instant she saw Trace without his shirt on, she knew just how blessed she really was. The man was utter perfection. All lean muscle covered by smooth skin. She could've easily stood there and ogled him for hours. In fact, she did that sometimes. When he offered to cook dinner, or the times he would work out in the home gym he'd set up on the first floor. Even when he was sleeping, she would unabashedly watch him.

"So, I assume shower sex was on today's agenda?" she teased.

"It is now."

Taking a moment to admire him, Marissa watched as he toed off his boots, kicking them to the side. She hoped they would survive the water, but at the moment, she really didn't care. Boots could be replaced, and truthfully, this was freaking hot.

Damn, he was beautiful.

"Come here, woman," Trace said, his voice gruff. He reached for her wrist and pulled her closer. "You keep looking at me like that and I'm gonna spontaneously combust."

"Looking at you like what?" She knew he enjoyed her innocent routine.

"Like I'm tiramisu."

She laughed. That was her favorite.

"I want your mouth on me," he mumbled against her lips, his hands sliding beneath her shirt, dipping into the waistband of her leggings. "I want to feel it wrap around my dick…"

A shiver of awareness coursed through her, making her nipples tighten and her insides clench hotly. She loved when Trace used his verbal seduction skills. Between the gruff tenor of his voice and the way he practically commanded her obedience … Marissa was hard-pressed to resist him.

Oh, who was she kidding? She rarely resisted him. Ever.

Pretending she was the smoking-hot vixen Trace deserved, Marissa grazed her lips over his shoulder, his chest, then lower. As he worked the button on his jeans free, she went to her knees, then trailed his fingers with her mouth as he lowered the denim over his hips.

"Have I told you how fucking perfect your mouth is?" he rasped when she took him in her mouth.

Yep, he'd told her. A million times. However, she would never get tired of hearing it.

Trace groaned, a deep, dark rumble that started in his chest and echoed through the bathroom. It spurred Marissa on, made her insides tremble with an ever-growing need for him.

His fingers tangled in her wet hair as he pushed into her mouth, retreating slowly. The slight sting that ignited on her scalp made her breathe deeply, her body coming to life instantly. She liked when he was rough with her. It was rare. And honestly, he wasn't really rough, but a little more forceful than usual. For the most part, he seemed to want to wrap her in silk and protect her, even from himself, so these moments when he wasn't completely aware of his dwindling self-control were the times she enjoyed most.

"Damn, baby…" he said softly. "Keep that up and I'm gonna lose it."

Well, they certainly couldn't have that. However, she didn't stop sucking him deep into her mouth, caressing the long, thick length of him with her tongue. Marissa knew he enjoyed this more than anything else.

"Oh, God, baby … yes. Do that thing with your tongue… Oh, fuck. That. Yes."

Marissa teased and tormented, knowing precisely what he liked because he always told her.

"Aww, damn… Can't take much more." Trace pumped his hips, fucking her mouth with gentle, deep strokes, his hands tangling in her hair.

Marissa moaned, watching him as he watched her. It was so erotic to watch him.

"Enough," he choked out, tugging at her hair, then reaching down to help her up.

Once she was back on her feet, Trace stripped the rest of their clothes from their bodies. But then it was her turn to be blinded by pleasure when he dropped to his knees, his tongue thrusting into her core. He lapped at her, fucked her with this tongue, and successfully drove her right out of her mind with mind-numbing pleasure. She never wanted him to stop.

So as he focused solely on driving her completely crazy with lust, the only thing Marissa could seem to do was hold on for dear life.

CHAPTER

9

TRACE WOULD BE THE FIRST TO ADMIT that making love to this woman was the absolute best way to pass the time. Didn't matter how or where, he got that same incredible high every damn time he was with her. The fact that she was so responsive only made him work harder to please her, loving the way her fingernails raked over his skin, her soft, sweet moans echoed in his ears.

"Trace… Need you inside me… Please."

He wanted to make her come with his mouth, at least once. Only then could he fuck her hard and fast. Even as she tried to push his head away, her fingers laced in his hair, Trace persisted, flicking his tongue over her clit while he pushed one finger inside her.

Her body trembled, and he held on to her with one arm, not wanting her to fall. He worked her, eating her pussy, loving every second of this until she was crying out his name. Instantly, he was up on his feet, his arms wrapped around her, his tongue thrusting into her mouth as he held her upright.

He wanted to make this last forever, but being inside her, feeling the smooth walls of her pussy contract around him, was the one thing he couldn't stop thinking about. It was the first thing he thought about when he woke up and the same thing he thought about throughout the day.

The way she moaned and sighed … yeah, that was pretty fucking awesome, too.

But the best part… The way Marissa kissed him. It was the same way every time. As though she couldn't get enough of him. It made his body hum, his blood heat, his heart race. He loved the way her tongue stroked his, exploring. The woman completed him in ways he'd never thought possible.

And the idea of her pregnant with his child…

It was almost too much. He could already picture her holding their son or daughter, singing softly, smiling so damn sweetly. He wanted that picture of perfection to come to life for them.

Gripping his aching dick, Trace guided himself to her entrance and slowly pushed inside. He had to grit his teeth as the sheer ecstasy consumed him, making his legs weak as her heat enveloped him.

He allowed her body to acclimate, giving her a chance to adjust to the intrusion before he began rocking into her, pulling back. Within seconds, he was slamming into her, holding her leg up so he could penetrate deeper.

"Trace…"

That one simple word said on a breathy whisper took him right to the brink and held him there, suspended on the razor-sharp edge of ecstasy as he continued to rock his hips, driving deep inside her, making her cry out his name over and over until…

"Yes!"

Trace groaned as he came in a furious rush while Marissa's arms squeezed his neck. They were still in the shower, the water cooling at this point, but it didn't matter, because holy hell, that was amazing.

"Is that how you're going to greet me every day when you come home?" she asked, leaning into him, her head resting on his shoulder. "Because I could totally live with that."

"I was thinking I wouldn't leave the house," he teased. "I'd simply stay lodged deep inside you from now until eternity."

"That could be interesting," she whispered, her muscles flexing around his cock, which was still buried inside her.

"Keep doing that and it's definitely going to get interesting." His dick pulsed with anticipation.

"Maybe a nap is in order."

"A nap?" Traced grinned, kissing her forehead as he pulled back. "I like the sound of that. And then, on to round two?"

"You're insatiable, you know that?"

"True. I'm not gonna deny it," he told her, regrettably pulling from her body.

"Of course you aren't."

THE NAP DIDN'T HAPPEN, BUT MARISSA HAD only been teasing. Sort of.

Instead, they had curled up on the couch and watched television for a couple of hours, something they rarely had the chance to do. And when Trace finally got up, Marissa had remained where she was, watching as he went to the kitchen to cook dinner. She had offered, but he'd insisted, and who in her right mind would refuse a man when he wanted to cook for her?

"Did you know Dani is officially back?" Trace asked when they were seated at the table a short while later.

"Courtney told me she showed up at Thanksgiving," Marissa admitted. "She said Dani was talking to Hunter."

Since Marissa hadn't seen the conversation take place, she had to assume it had been when she and Trace had slipped out to the garage.

Trace nodded.

Marissa sensed that it hadn't gone as well as she would've hoped. "Please tell me he's not gonna run off again?" She knew it wasn't easy on their family when Hunter had disappeared the first time.

"He can't outrun his feelings for her," Trace stated.

"No, he can't. But he can face them." Marissa watched her husband. "Has he tried to talk to her? *Really* talk?"

Trace shrugged. "He won't talk about her."

"Still?"

"Still."

Wanting to change the subject, Marissa opted to talk about work. "Did you talk to RT about staying in town until Christmas?"

"He's good with it. Hunter agreed to take any out-of-town assignments for now."

"Of course he did." Still running, Marissa knew. Eventually, it would all catch up with him, but that was the way it worked.

However, the good thing was that Trace would be home, or close anyway. Not that Marissa had a lot on her to-do list. Her Christmas shopping was complete. That was one of the perks of being so organized. She had started planning back in July, and as she found things for each of the members of their families, Marissa had purchased and even wrapped the gifts, storing them in the closet in the guest bedroom.

Now, it was a matter of enjoying every minute leading up to the big day. Of course, with nothing else to keep her busy these days, she was inundated with thoughts of a baby. She had forced herself not to get ahead of herself this time, though. She didn't want to jinx anything. Marissa knew that pregnancies didn't always happen instantly, no matter how badly a couple wanted to conceive. She had friends who had spent years trying both naturally and with fertility treatments. It sometimes took time. So, she opted to keep a positive outlook, knowing that things would happen if they were meant to happen.

That didn't mean that she wasn't saying an extra prayer every single day in hopes that it would happen sooner rather than later.

CHAPTER 10

Monday, December 19th

TRACE WASN'T PARTICULARLY FOND OF THE OFFICE Christmas party, yet he attended it every year. It was always the same. Lunch catered in, desserts brought by employees, and someone always suggesting they do the white-elephant gifts. This year they went a little crazy, bringing in Italian food. Granted, it was a hell of a lot better than turkey and dressing as far as Trace was concerned. There were piles of cookies, rows of pies, and several multilayer things that he didn't dare go near. And yes, the white-elephant exchange had taken place. Once again, everyone had attempted to buy the most inappropriate gift that would embarrass the recipient.

As usual, that had worked and had been immensely entertaining. Last year, RT had been the one who had blushed to the roots of his hair. This year, Kye Sterling seemed to be the focus. Trace wasn't sure if that was because he was the relatively new guy or because the women seemed to ooh and ahh over the blond-haired, blue-eyed giant of a man every time he came into the office. Not that he was there often. Hunter seemed to have that man on a leash, directing his every move.

It wasn't that Trace's brother had technically partnered with Kye, but they were working together. Hunter seemed to be the one who had taken Kye under his wing. Or maybe there was something else at work there that Trace didn't quite understand. He'd noticed the way Kye looked at Hunter from time to time. If he wasn't mistaken, there was some sort of deep admiration that lit up Kye's face every time he caught sight of Hunter. How that worked, Trace had no idea, but it wasn't his place to figure it out, either.

Shaking his head at the thought, Trace focused on the conversation taking place in front of him. Jayden Brooks, their beloved receptionist, was currently in an all-out argument with Conner over the best hotels in Las Vegas. How they'd managed to get on the topic was beyond him.

"Caesar's Palace is by far the nicest place on the strip," Jayden insisted.

"I disagree," Conner countered. "The Aria is much nicer."

"What do you know?" Jayden retorted, laughing. "When's the last time you even took a vacation?"

Trace expected Conner to get quiet, the way he usually did. The man hadn't been the same since his wife had been brutally murdered years ago. The only thing he seemed to do was work and spend a relatively small amount of time with his daughter.

"I'll prove it to you," Conner declared. "I'll take you to Vegas and show you."

Okay, even Trace noticed the way everyone's jaw practically hit the floor with that proposal.

"You're on, tough guy," Jayden stated firmly. "I'll prove I know more than you."

When Conner laughed, Trace quickly looked away. He wanted to hear his brother laugh like that more. He didn't care who was putting that smile on his face, as long as someone was. As he turned, he made eye contact with RT and they both shrugged.

Whatever was at play there…

Who knew what it was, but Trace damn sure wasn't going to interfere.

MARISSA DIDN'T USUALLY ATTEND THE SNIPER 1 Security Christmas parties. Not because she wasn't invited, because, for whatever reason, she was every single year. It didn't seem to matter that she didn't work for the company—despite her family pestering her about it for years and years—they always extended her an invitation.

But since she and Trace had gotten married, she'd attended because he had asked her to. Honestly, these gatherings weren't much different than most of her family get-togethers. So much love in one place among those who were related by blood and those who were family by association. If she really thought about it, Marissa had to admit that she loved every minute of it.

"You havin' a good time, kiddo?" her father asked when he came to stand beside her, his arm coming around her shoulder.

Bryce Trexler, at sixty-one, was an imposing figure. At six four, he was still in tremendous shape, and it was obvious by looking at him.

"Of course. You?"

Bryce smiled brightly, his blue eyes twinkling. "Always."

She peered up at him. "So, you think you might really retire next year? Or is it one of those things you'll keep saying until one day it possibly comes true?"

He'd been saying it for so long no one believed he would follow through.

Her father chuckled. "Hey, I'm working my way out little by little. Your brother's got things under control."

Marissa searched the room until she found RT. He was laughing at something Z said.

Her father was right. RT had taken the reins of the company nicely. Everyone loved him; there seemed to be no animosity between him and any of the Kogans. Considering the company was owned fifty-fifty between Bryce and Casper, it could've been a knock-down, drag-out when it came time to assign someone to take the lead. Instead, everyone had seemed to back off, and RT had walked right into the role. It was working out well.

"And you?" Bryce asked. "You plannin' to come work for us finally?"

"Not a chance," she told him. "I'm gonna keep doing what I'm doing."

Being that she was a political blogger, things had slowed down for her considerably since the presidential election was over. The past year had been a brutal battle, and she was thankful it was over.

"Of course you are." Her father kissed her on the top of her head. "Just remember, if you ever get tired of that shit, there's always a place for you here."

"I know, Daddy." And she did.

As much as she loved these people, she didn't want to be in the fold of Sniper 1 Security. She respected what they did, but it wasn't her thing.

"You ready for some cookies? I see Z has his eye on them. If we don't hurry, they'll be gone before we get the chance," Bryce teased, nudging her forward.

"Well, we can't have that, now can we?"

CHAPTER 11

*Wednesday, December 21*st

TRACE WAS SITTING AT HIS DESK IN his home office when he heard Marissa's footsteps on the concrete floor outside the door. He peered up just as she stepped into the doorway.

"You busy?" she asked, holding a cup of coffee to her lips.

He noticed she was still wearing her robe, although she'd gotten up at least two hours ago. That was very unlike her. She was usually dressed and flitting around the house or sitting with her nose buried in her laptop shortly after she awoke.

"Nope," he said. Trace had long ago made a personal rule that Marissa came before anything else. "Why? Something on your mind?"

Marissa padded into the room, setting her coffee mug on the windowsill before making her way over to him. Trace leaned back in his chair and watched as she perched on the edge of his desk.

"You weren't in bed when I woke up," she said, toying with the tie on her robe.

"I know. Just dealing with some crap at work. Nothing major."

"That acquisition thing RT asked you to look into?"

Trace nodded. Sniper 1 Security had been approached by a small security consulting firm, mostly corporate and residential, that had fallen on hard times financially. Because they were established and well-respected within the industry, RT wanted to look at the possibility of buying them out and absorbing them. Trace had offered to do some digging into their financials.

"Well, if you've got a minute…"

Trace looked up at his wife, noticing when she parted the robe, creamy flesh peeking out.

A minute? Hell, he had the rest of the day.

"I've always got a minute for you," he told her, sitting up straight and moving his chair so that he was in front of her.

He helped her up onto his desk, keeping her directly in front of him.

Trace allowed his palms to trail up the smooth skin on her thighs, pushing the robe farther apart so he could get a glimpse of the incredible body beneath. He noticed Marissa watching him, clearly happy with the way things were going.

Taking his time, Trace teased with his hands, caressing her, enjoying the sleek skin against his palms. The woman stole his breath.

"This is what I wanted for Christmas," he told her, grinning.

"It's not Christmas yet, silly."

No, it wasn't.

"Spread your legs," he urged, nudging her thighs apart with his forearms.

Marissa obliged him, opening herself up to him. Trace took what she was offering, smiling to himself as he admired the soft, glistening folds of her pussy. He readjusted her feet, putting them on the arms of the chair and pulling her closer to the edge of the desk, bringing her pussy right in line with his mouth.

He separated her folds with his thumbs, then stroked her with his tongue.

"Trace…"

Damn, he loved the raspy tone of her voice, husky and so fucking sweet when she was turned on.

He continued to stroke and caress, maintaining a leisurely pace. He could honestly do this all fucking day long. Her sweetness against his tongue ratcheted up his need, but he ignored it. His sole focus was pleasuring his wife.

Minutes passed while Trace was lost in her, feasting on her until Marissa's fingers twined in his hair, tugging his head. He refused to give in until she gave him what he was seeking, though, so he pretended not to notice while increasing the friction of his tongue, flicking her clit relentlessly until she was gasping and moaning.

Only when she came did he finally look up to see her staring back at him, blue eyes glazed.

"Inside me," she whispered.

On his desk? Damn. Was it his fucking birthday?

Standing up, Trace pushed his sweat pants down his thighs and took a step forward, aligning his cock with her entrance and slowly pushing inside. No need to waste time. He was more than willing to give her what she asked for.

He gripped Marissa's hips, holding her still so he could watch as his dick disappeared into the warmth of her body, withdrew. His shaft glistened with her juices, which only tormented him, his dick throbbing.

The friction was incredible. He didn't rush, slowly thrusting in as deep as he could go before retreating. Again and again and again. Only when her cries sounded more urgent, her orgasm hanging just out of reach, did he speed up. His hips pumped faster as he pushed his thumb against her clit, stroking in circles, applying enough pressure to make her whimper.

"Come for me, Marissa. Come all over my cock, baby," he crooned softly, keeping his tone smooth, soft.

"Close," she whispered. "So close."

Shifting slightly, Trace lifted her legs over his arms, changing the angle of penetration as he pushed in harder, deeper. He punched his hips forward, withdrew slowly.

"Oh, yes… Like that … Trace…"

He felt her body tighten around him, her muscles locking onto his cock, milking him as he tried to hold out, desperate to send her over first. It didn't take long before Marissa was crying out his name, her head thrown back, pussy squeezing him.

Seeing her in the throes of a powerful orgasm sent him right over the edge.

MARISSA WAS WALKING ON A CLOUD, OR it felt that way. She wasn't sure what it was. Maybe it was the fact that Christmas was only a couple of days away, or perhaps because Trace had been home and she was getting to spend a lot of time with him.

Whatever it was, she hoped the feeling didn't go away.

As it was, she was hard-pressed to keep herself busy. That usually wasn't a problem, but her mind seemed to be focused on one thing: the pregnancy test sitting in the cabinet beneath the sink in their bathroom.

No, she hadn't taken it yet. Part of her feared it was too soon. The other part feared that it would be negative and she would be disappointed. She'd been telling herself that it wouldn't matter. They had all the time in the world to keep trying. But the truth of the matter was she'd gotten her hopes up.

She felt different. Then again, that could've been a mental thing thanks to her wishful thinking.

"Hey."

Marissa spun around to see her husband watching her from across the room. She smiled.

"Are you okay?"

"Perfect." And that really was the truth. "Just trying to think of something to do."

"I thought maybe we could go cruise some neighborhoods, check out the Christmas lights."

Smiling, Marissa nodded. She loved doing that and Trace knew it. He would never choose to do it, otherwise, if it weren't for her.

"That would be great." Plus, it would take her mind off everything else.

Even if for just a little while.

CHAPTER 12

Sunday, December 25th

SINCE HIS SEXY WIFE GOT IT INTO her head to sneak a peek at all of his little surprises, Trace had been forced to get creative. Although thanks to her sneaky ways, she knew what each slip of paper in the Advent calendar said, Trace had managed to mix them up every morning before Marissa had a chance to pretend she didn't already know. That had worked for the past couple of weeks, but now that they were down to only one day left—today—it wasn't quite so simple.

As it was, for the past few days, he'd had to get even more imaginative by changing them altogether. And yes, when it came to their sex life, the past few weeks had been adventurous to say the least. He had managed to blindfold his sweet wife, tie her up, even make love to her out on the balcony (at night, with the lights off so they had the illusion of privacy). Then, there had been the time in his truck at the Sniper 1 Security office, down in the parking garage of the warehouse, once in the bathroom at his parents' house, and his personal favorite, on his desk right here in his home office. He would never be able to work another minute in this room without thinking about how she'd come apart with his mouth fastened to her pussy.

Damn.

Just thinking about it made his dick roar to life. He remembered how Marissa had insisted that it was possible to have too much sex. She'd given a good argument, too. Sure, being a male, he had doubted that wholeheartedly, and the truth was, he was right. There was no such thing as too much sex. Not when it came to Marissa.

Not in his mind, anyway. As for her … yeah, it was quite possible that he'd worn her out a time or two. She was starting to push him off, which was why he'd planned for a romantic night last night. Simple. Sweet. That had been his goal. He had cooked her dinner, dined by candlelight, then swept her off her feet and made love to her right in their bed for as long as she'd let him.

But today was the last day, and honestly, he didn't have a clue what to do.

Although he would never shy away from sex, Trace knew that this wasn't all about that. It was about the connection they had, the love they shared. Marissa was his entire world. The love of his life. He would do anything to make her happy. Anything.

Since today was Christmas Day, they would be spending it together. The two of them. Tonight they would spend the evening with the family, a huge get-together at Marissa's parents' house. He looked forward to it every year, and he knew Marissa did as well. But with a huge family gathering came a tremendous amount of stress. So he wanted today to be a relaxing day for the two of them, right up until dinner.

"Trace? Will you come here for a minute?"

He turned in his chair, then pushed away from his desk.

The instant he set foot into the living room, his jaw dropped to the floor.

There, wearing nothing but a pair of teeny tiny panties and a big red bow, was his incredibly beautiful wife standing beneath a sprig of mistletoe dangling from the beam in the ceiling. He even registered the fact that she was holding something behind her back, but he couldn't focus on that with the sight of her naked form.

"I wanted to give you your Christmas present," she said, her voice raspy, seductive.

Okay, so maybe she wasn't as worn out as he'd thought.

"If it's you, then this is the best present ever."

She smiled. "Well, that's part of the gift."

He forced his feet to move, closing the distance between them. "And the other part?" Not that he really cared about any other part.

Marissa held out a small wrapped box. "Open it."

Without waiting, Trace tore off the paper, then lifted the lid and peered down into the box. For the first time in his life, he was speechless.

There, nestled in white tissue paper, was a...

Pregnancy test.

"It's positive," she whispered.

He looked up, and with blurry eyes, he noticed tears in her eyes.

"I honestly didn't expect it to happen," she said hurriedly. "Not this soon anyway, but..."

Setting the box on the counter, Trace pulled Marissa into his arms and buried his face in her neck. He didn't try to hold back the tears, letting them fall, his happiness overwhelming him. For whatever reason, Trace had thought it would take months to get pregnant. He had tried not to get his hopes up, but the truth was, he had. And this...

"Best Christmas present ever," she whispered, cradling his head. "I love you."

"God, I love you, too, baby." More than she could possibly imagine.

"Is Z INSISTING THAT WE PLAY HOLIDAY charades again?" Courtney whispered, exasperation ringing in her tone.

Then again, they had played it three times already.

Marissa grinned. "It looks like it."

"That man never tires of that game."

True. He didn't. Marissa's brother-in-law was the life of the party, no doubt about it. And he was always trying to make things livelier. Even if his team won every single time, no one seemed to tire of trying to guess the name of the holiday song that one person was acting out. They'd learned last year that if you wanted to win, having Z on your team was imperative.

"So … any news on the baby front?" Courtney asked, her voice so low Marissa hardly heard her.

But she had heard. And she shook her head. "Not yet," she lied easily.

Right now, she and Trace agreed that they would keep this a secret for a little while. Considering she hadn't been to the doctor to confirm that the pregnancy test was accurate, she didn't want everyone getting too excited. Even if it meant lying to her best friend. For now.

Marissa glanced over at Courtney. "What about you? Are you and Max planning to have a baby anytime soon?"

Courtney's cheeks reddened, making Marissa pause. Courtney never blushed. The girl was always so out and open about everything. At times, Marissa thought it was impossible for the woman to be embarrassed. Not that she was embarrassed, but she was certainly hiding something.

Then it dawned on her. "Oh, my God!"

"Shh!" Courtney slapped her hand over Marissa's mouth. "Don't tell anyone yet."

"How far along are you?"

Courtney's smile widened. "Almost three months."

There was no way she could keep quiet with that. "And you didn't tell me?"

"Didn't tell her what?" Conner asked, peering over at them.

"Yeah, what are you talking about?" Z inquired. "Share with the rest of us. It's Christmas."

Marissa watched as Courtney peered over at her husband. Max smiled and gave a barely discernible nod.

"We're pregnant," Courtney announced, her eyes bright with unshed tears.

And just like that, the house erupted in laughter and cheers. Everyone was congratulating Courtney and Max. Marissa couldn't wipe the smile off her face. She was so happy for her friend. And to think, they would be pregnant at the same time.

Trace squeezed Marissa's shoulder gently, and she reached up to pat his hand. Yep, they had a little secret of their own, a Christmas gift shared between the two of them. In a couple of months, they would share the news, but tonight she would let Courtney have her time in the sun. She deserved it.

And by this time next year, there would be babies in the house during Christmas dinner. It had been so long since they'd had a baby around. With Conner's daughter now fifteen, it had been far too long.

Yep, it was safe to say their families were growing.

They were blessed. Truly blessed.

 To Give and to Receive

Teague Carter and Hudson Ballard

from *Speechless*

CHAPTER
1

Monday, December 12

"No." Teague Carter grinned, backing up. "No, no, no." He turned to his dog, who was obediently sitting on the floor. "Sic him, Charger."

Hudson grinned.

"How is it he's my dog yet he listens more to you?"

Hudson was standing there, holding up one finger, signaling for Charger to sit, and the dog obeyed him. This was the dog Hudson had gotten for him as an emotional support dog. Charger should ignore Hudson, especially since Teague had been trying to teach him that trick for months now.

Right.

Like anyone could ignore Hudson. Hell, the man didn't speak, yet he had a bigger presence than anyone Teague had ever known.

"Get away from me," Teague grumbled on a laugh, skirting the couch and putting it between him and the big man stalking him. "I'm not going with you. No way."

Teague's gaze dropped to Hudson's hands as the man began signing his response.

Sure you are. I will throw you over my shoulder and carry you out if I have to.

Teague wouldn't put it past him. In fact, Hudson had done it before. About a month ago. When Teague had refused to go over to Cam and Gannon's for an impromptu dinner one night. It was no secret that Teague didn't care to get close to a lot of people. This thing between him and Hudson was an exception to his rule.

Still, he laughed, keeping his eyes on the big guy. An idea came to him.

Hudson's eyes widened and he held up his hands. *No. Don't you dare.*

Like he took orders from the man. Teague smirked, pulling his shirt up and over his head, then tossing it to the couch. He toed off his shoes and went for the button on his jeans. Hudson definitely couldn't force him to go to the Christmas tree farm if he was naked, now could he?

Before he could get his jeans unbuttoned, the big guy was on him, knocking him to the couch, making him laugh even harder.

"Oh, fuck," Teague moaned when Hudson came down over him. "I'm still not going. I don't care what you do to me." Sure, it was a bit of a dare. So what?

Although he'd thought stripping naked was a good idea, Teague should've known better with Hudson here. The man made him hard as iron with just a look. There were days he walked around with a perpetual boner, waiting for any crumb the guy would give him. Yes, Hudson liked to hold out on him as punishment. Of course, when Hudson finally caved and gave Teague what he needed, the timing didn't matter. He craved the man. Day, night. Twenty-four seven, in fact.

Strong hands slid over Teague's chest as Hudson moved closer, pushing his thigh between Teague's legs. Hudson's hands pressed against his abdomen, his thumbs gliding upward, between his ribs, over his chest.

"You play dirty," Teague accused, already breathing hard.

130

Hudson's emerald-green eyes glittered with heat and desire. Teague had seen that look a million times before. Ever since he'd succumbed to Hudson months ago, giving in to the inevitable lust that he inspired in him. He knew that Hudson would eventually get his way. That Teague would end up going with him to pick out a stupid, soon-to-be-dead tree, but until then, he would definitely take what was being offered. However, Teague wasn't about to make it easy for him. He lived for this shit right here.

Teague heard the dog whimper, probably wondering why they'd stopped playing.

"Charger, lie down," he whispered loud enough for the dog to hear, never looking away from Hudson. "You're gonna make me go, aren't you?"

Hudson nodded.

"Why?" That was a question he really wanted an answer to. "Why do we have to have a Christmas tree?"

Teague didn't celebrate Christmas. In fact, he didn't celebrate any holiday. Ever. No birthdays, graduations, and certainly not the time-honored traditions brought on by people who believed in shit Teague didn't believe in. Sure, a couple of the foster homes he'd been raised in had tried to include him in their festivities, but the fucked up kid he'd once been hadn't cared to participate.

Until this year, he'd even managed to keep himself apart from the guys for these ridiculous get-togethers. However, they'd somehow managed to wrangle him over to Cam and Gannon's for Thanksgiving a few weeks ago. He thought that would've been enough to satisfy them, but clearly Teague had been wrong.

Being that he was mute, Hudson used American Sign Language to communicate, and during their time together, Teague had become more fluent. Enough that he knew what Hudson was saying, but he didn't need the man to sign his words; he already knew what the answer was.

Because I want you to.

That was obviously one of Hudson's favorite responses. It made Teague smile.

"What do I get out of the deal?"

Hudson's devilish smirk told Teague everything he wanted to know. And when Hudson pinched Teague's nipples, his body went up in flames.

"Oh, fuck," he moaned softly, pushing his chest up, silently begging for more. He dug his head into the pillow, offering himself up to Hudson. He didn't care what the man did to him as long as he didn't stop.

Hudson leaned down, sliding his tongue across one of the tormented discs, turning Teague to putty in his hands.

"Don't stop," Teague mumbled when Hudson lifted his head. "Please don't stop."

Hudson laved Teague's other nipple, gently biting him with his teeth. Fire shot from his nipple to his dick, intensifying the ache that seemed to live inside him day and night.

Unable to help himself, Teague ground his throbbing dick against Hudson's rock-hard thigh, trying to bring himself some sort of relief. As much as he liked where this was going, he had a good feeling about how it was going to end. Hudson would give him what he wanted, what he needed, but he was going to make Teague work for it.

Which meant...

Hudson got to his feet, his fingers unbuttoning his own jeans before shoving them down his hips. Teague got an eyeful of Hudson's impressive cock, the thick, slightly curved shaft, the broad, bulbous head. His mouth watered with the need to taste him, to push him past his breaking point with merely his lips and tongue.

Suck me.

Yep, he'd known what was coming, and unfortunately, it wasn't going to be him.

Not yet, anyway.

What Teague didn't understand was why that didn't bother him quite as much as it should.

HUDSON BALLARD WOULD MOVE HEAVEN AND EARTH for the man lying before him. He would do whatever it took to please Teague, to push him to experience life in ways he'd never done before. And no, he wasn't above using sex to get what he wanted. After all, he knew it was Teague's preferred method.

Back in the beginning, Hudson had held out, refusing to give in to Teague's needs. Not because he hadn't wanted it but because he'd wanted all of Teague. Not just his body. It had taken some time and a hell of a lot of patience, but Hudson had ended up with the one thing that meant the most to him. Teague's love. The physical aspect of their relationship was extraordinary, but the emotional side was so much better.

And just like any time Teague pushed him, Hudson wasn't going to give him everything he wanted just yet.

Hudson took himself in hand, gently stroking his dick while he stared down at the man he loved more than life itself. He offered a smile, then pointed to his cock, urging Teague to get on with it. He knew Teague needed to be dominated, which worked so fucking well for Hudson because he enjoyed the hell out of dominating the man.

He watched as Teague slowly sat up, his stomach muscles flexing, the hard ridge of his erection pressing against his zipper. The man needed something, and Hudson fully intended to give it to him, but not until later. Right now, this was all he had to offer. Although it seemed downright selfish, Hudson had learned what Teague wanted, what he craved, and strangely enough, it often involved forcing the man's submission.

Hudson used his hands to communicate. *I said suck me.*

There was a hint of defiance in Teague's blue eyes, but Hudson wasn't worried. Teague would do as instructed because he wanted to. Hudson couldn't hold back his dominating nature, and Teague couldn't resist it. They were meant for each other.

When Teague leaned forward, Hudson guided his dick right to those sweet lips, gently swiping the head over the softness before urging Teague's mouth open. And when Teague relented, wrapping his mouth around him, Hudson wished he could speak. He would've groaned to show just how damn good that felt. Since he couldn't produce sound, he had to communicate with touch.

133

Reaching for Teague's head, he slid one hand in Teague's hair, curling his fingers in the silky blond strands, then using his other hand to cup Teague's jaw, sliding his thumb over Teague's neck lovingly.

He forced his cock deeper into the warmth of the man's mouth, loving the way Teague gave him what he needed in return. He knew Teague wanted to be fucked, but Hudson had learned how to play this game with him.

Teague was a complicated man. He'd been through hell, always keeping himself apart from everyone else, feeling left out and alone despite the few friends he'd had, despite the way he had immersed himself in meaningless sex. It wasn't until Teague had tried to commit suicide that Hudson had realized the extent of the man's problems. After extensive counseling in a hospital, Teague had come out the other side a different man. A stronger man.

A man Hudson loved beyond reason, beyond words.

Hudson tightened his fingers in Teague's hair, tugging hard enough to show how much Teague was affecting him. He loved the man's mouth. Then again, he loved every damn thing about him. His smart mouth, his constant need to resist everything, his need to be held, to be loved. Hudson loved it all. Good and bad.

He began thrusting his hips forward, pushing deeper while still cupping Teague's mouth, urging him with his hands, *telling* him what he wanted, what he needed by touch.

Teague moaned, making sparks shoot straight to Hudson's balls. The vibrations were incredible, his body humming with the pleasure coursing through him.

Hudson took a step closer, releasing Teague's jaw as he forced Teague back. He continued until Teague was leaning against the back cushions and Hudson, with one foot planted on the couch, was practically fucking his mouth, driving deeper, taking what he needed.

Their eyes met and held, Teague's gaze hot with lust. The man was so fucking sexy, sometimes Hudson swore he could come simply by looking at him.

He gave in to his need for release, pumping his hips while Teague took him as deep into his throat as he could. Fire sizzled in his bloodstream, driving him higher and higher. When Teague's hands gripped Hudson's ass, pulling him closer, he lost his grip on his control, coming hard and fast, right down Teague's throat.

He fell on top of Teague, guiding him back down to the couch, kissing him, tasting himself on Teague's lips. Hudson cupped Teague's head with one hand, covering his neck with the other, holding him in place, ensuring Teague knew just how crazy he made him.

"I don't suppose it's my turn," Teague mumbled when Hudson pulled back a short while later.

Hudson smirked as he pushed up onto his knees.

Not yet, no. But it will be. I promise.

"Promises, promises." Teague's teasing tone made his heart swell.

Be careful what you wish for.

The blue in Teague's eyes glowed brightly. "You don't scare me. I can take anything you can dish out."

Hudson knew that to be true.

Another thing he loved about the man.

CHAPTER 2

"WHY ARE WE DOING THIS AGAIN?" TEAGUE asked, grimacing as they wandered through the endless rows of trees. He bent down to pat Charger's head, letting the dog know how good he was doing. If the dog was anything like him, he wanted to be anywhere but here. Granted, Charger was usually the happy-go-lucky kind, content to be just about anywhere.

But a tree farm? Really?

Teague didn't like the smell of … whatever the hell the trees were … but he hoped that was because they were in a condensed area. Otherwise, he didn't really mind it. He liked that Hudson wanted a Christmas tree. It was a new thing for him, certainly not something he would've come up with himself, but admittedly, the idea was growing on him. When it came down to it, Teague wanted what Hudson wanted. He simply wanted to make the guy happy, and if decorating a tree for Christmas made him happy, so be it. He'd gotten used to all of Hudson's quirks these past few months, and he honestly wouldn't want to change a thing.

Hudson responded with: *Because it is what we do for Christmas.*

We.

Every time Hudson said "we," Teague felt a strange sensation in his chest. Not completely foreign, because he'd felt it many times before in recent months, and he was getting used to it. It was love, he knew. Something he'd managed not to feel for his entire life. Not until this man, anyway. When it came to Hudson, Teague couldn't help but feel it. The man had saved his life. Not only because he'd literally saved him by fishing him out of the water, but also because Hudson had given him something to look forward to, someone to depend on, a home.

"They all look the same," he grumbled, biting back the urge to smile. "What are you looking for?"

Hudson shrugged.

Teague followed him, Charger at his side as they wound their way through the tent-covered area. He made sure to sigh dramatically a time or two, ensuring that Hudson knew he was put out. Not that he really was, but he definitely looked forward to Hudson making it up to him later.

Finally, Hudson stopped in front of a tree they'd passed at least ten times already.

This one.

"Perfect." Teague didn't see the difference between it and all the others. "What do we do now?"

Hudson nodded toward the man who worked there.

Sighing heavily, Teague turned away from Hudson, smiling to himself. He led Charger over to the guy.

"We'd like a tree. Seeing that you're selling some, I guess we're in the right place. I don't know what it is about the damn thing, but he's finally picked one out." Teague jerked his thumb in Hudson's direction. "And he'd like that one."

"Nice choice."

Again, Teague didn't see the difference between it and any of the others, but he nodded because the guy seemed pleased with their selection.

Of course, it would've been far too easy for the guy to wrap it up and send them on their way. No, after Hudson chopped the damn thing down with a hacksaw—which was unbearably sexy, he would admit—the guy who worked there wanted to chat, and once he realized Hudson couldn't communicate verbally, he looked to Teague to answer for him. Teague did his best not to be rude, but *come on*. Buying a tree should not take a solid hour.

When the guy finally did start netting the thing up and wrapping rope around it, Teague wandered off, forcing an end to the conversation. He let Charger sniff everything in sight before returning to see them heading toward the parking lot.

Twenty minutes later, the tree was secured in the bed of Hudson's truck, Charger in the back seat, and they were back on the road.

"So, is it my turn yet?" Teague asked, glancing over at the man behind the wheel.

Hudson's dark eyebrows lifted questioningly.

"For my blow job? You know, turnabout is fair play, and I was a good little boy, going to the tree place and all. I think it's only fair."

Hudson's grin grew wider, which was exactly what Teague had been going for.

They pulled up to a red light and Hudson lifted his hands from the wheel.

Only one more place to go.

"What?" Teague pretended to be outraged. "Where the hell are we going now?"

He had to watch Hudson's hands closely as he spelled out his answer.

O-r-n-a-m-e-n-t-s.

Teague glanced out the window and muttered, "Son of a bitch," under his breath. "That damn blow job better be fucking worth it."

Of course, he smiled.

But not so Hudson could see it.

After all, Teague damn sure didn't want Hudson to know he would gladly follow him anywhere.

Hudson purposely took his time strolling down aisle after aisle of holiday decorations. He wasn't looking for anything specific; he was simply trying to see how far he could push Teague. The man lived to torment him, so Hudson figured it was only fair to pay him back.

Had he not been with Teague, Hudson would've grabbed the first few things he saw and jetted out of the store in less than ten minutes. As it was, Hudson had been at it for thirty minutes now, and he was surprised Teague hadn't gone apeshit yet. The countdown was on, though, and he figured the volcano that was Teague Carter would blow any time now.

"What's wrong with that shit?" Teague grumbled when they passed another section of silver and gold ornaments.

An older woman cast a reproachful look at them, but Teague paid her no mind.

Hudson simply shook his head and kept walking.

"Jesus Christ, Charger. He's worse than a woman."

Grinning, he stopped and pretended to consider some brightly colored glass ornaments. They had feathers attached to them and were, quite frankly, hideous.

"No fucking way," Teague mumbled, keeping his voice low. "Get serious, would ya?"

And the kid didn't think he contributed to this sort of thing.

Hudson slowly pivoted to face Teague. He smiled down at the man, then grabbed his shirt and tugged him closer, kissing him right there in the store. He knew there was no one around to see them, but he wasn't sure if Teague knew that.

Teague didn't pull away. The man was obviously okay with public displays of affection. He never seemed to mind where they were or who might see them. Hudson liked that about him. He didn't want to hide their relationship, and he didn't have to with Teague.

When he pulled back, he nodded his head toward the end of the aisle, then went back to one of the first aisles they'd gone down.

"You're serious right now? We couldn't have stopped here thirty minutes ago?"

Hudson filled the basket with lights and ornaments, tinsel, and other miscellaneous crap to decorate their apartments. Fifteen minutes later, with all the stuff loaded into the bed of the truck and Charger and Teague finally inside, Hudson hopped behind the wheel and turned in the direction of the marina.

It didn't take long to get back, nor did it take long to unload the stuff and carry it upstairs. When they were finally finished, Hudson headed over to his apartment. They'd pretty much lived together since Teague got out of treatment, still inhabiting both apartments, but they'd turned Teague's into the room where they watched television and had dinner, while Hudson's side was where they spent the nights. The only real difference in the appearance was the fact that Hudson had added a few things here and there—pictures, whatnots—to spruce it up and make it appear as though someone lived there and didn't simply sleep there.

Although there were times he considered finding them something more suitable—a house where Charger would have a yard, maybe—Hudson hadn't seriously pursued it. The living arrangements were working for them. While it was obvious Dare, Cam, and Roan preferred houses, Hudson didn't mind living over the marina office. It was close to work. Plus, it allowed Hudson to sneak off with Teague whenever he wanted. Well, whenever he wasn't slipping into the small office in the boat repair shop, that was. He happened to enjoy those times equally.

Hudson heard Teague instructing Charger to lie down, followed by the sound of footsteps. He pretended to be looking for something.

"My turn," Teague announced from behind him.

Hudson turned to look at him. Again, he pretended not to know what Teague was talking about when, in reality, he'd spent the better part of the afternoon thinking of nothing but Teague and the fact that he wanted to get the man naked.

He admired Teague's sleek, muscular form as Teague not so gracefully stripped his clothes from his body. First his shirt, then his shoes and socks, followed by his jeans. The kid turned him on like nothing else ever could. And no, he didn't really think of Teague as a kid, but he'd always referred to him that way. Considering there was nearly ten years' difference in their ages, he figured he was entitled. But Teague certainly wasn't a kid by any stretch of the imagination.

"Do you plan to finish what you started earlier?" Teague asked, hands on his lean hips, his cock bobbing eagerly between his legs. "Or do I finally get to be in charge?"

The thought of Teague topping him appealed to Hudson in a way he'd never thought possible. He had yet to succumb to the desire, though. Maybe it was a mental block or something. Yes, he'd been thinking about it a lot, but he hadn't gotten to the point he was ready to give in yet. When Teague had initially mentioned it, Hudson thought the kid was joking, but he'd soon learned that Teague was quite interested.

And yes, Hudson had every intention of giving in, but he was waiting for the right moment. It would present itself; he had no doubt. Today wasn't the day, though.

What about dinner?

"I've got your dinner right here," Teague retorted, pointing to his dick. "Then, if you're still hungry after you suck me off, we can eat. Well, after you fuck me. I'll even cook."

Hudson loved this man. Loved every wild thing about him.

Well, in that case…

Of course, Teague didn't move. He remained standing there, sinfully naked, all but teasing Hudson with the way his dick continued to swell, lengthening as he watched.

Yeah, it was definitely time to give Teague what he needed.

CHAPTER 3

TEAGUE NOTICED THE MOMENT HUDSON GAVE IN. It was etched right there on his handsome face, flashing brightly in his green eyes. The man could mask his expression like no one Teague had ever known, but there were times, like now, when he could be read like a book.

An erotic novel, in fact.

Teague had learned to read him during the months they'd been together. He knew just how far he had to push to get Hudson where he wanted him to go. No, he didn't think he had figured the man out, but he had him pegged at certain times.

Like right now.

Hudson used his finger to signal for Teague to turn around.

Okay, so this was new.

Well, not entirely. Hudson was often behind him when they were fucking, but usually Teague was on the couch, the bed, or even against the wall. Right now, he was standing in the middle of the room.

However, he wasn't the kind to argue when he was clearly going to get what he wanted, so he turned around and faced the open door that led out into the hallway between the apartments and waited.

And waited.

He didn't turn back because he knew that was what Hudson wanted. Instead, he palmed his dick roughly, ready to pleasure himself.

The giant hand that instantly wrapped around his wrist made him jump.

Teague glanced over his shoulder at Hudson. Damn, the big man was already naked, which made this moment that much hotter. Thankfully, Hudson didn't seem to be in the mood to make Teague wait all damn night. He'd done it before. More than once, actually. The guy was notorious for dragging it out until Teague thought his head would explode. Both of them.

"Aww, damn," he hissed, leaning back against Hudson when the man's hand moved from Teague's wrist to his dick. "Fuck, that feels good."

Hudson's lips found his neck, sliding slowly up and down, moving in time with the exquisite hand job. Teague could feel Hudson's cock pressing against his ass, and he was tempted to bend over to make this go faster. Only, if he did that, he knew Hudson would stop stroking him, and right now, that was what he wanted most.

Teague reached over his shoulder and grabbed Hudson's head, turning his own so he could meet the man's mouth with his. The kiss was slow, seductive, exactly what the moment called for. Unfortunately, Hudson's hand did drop from his cock, but when Teague turned to face him, he didn't think too much about it. His hands slid over the smooth skin of Hudson's chest, while Hudson gripped Teague's hair roughly.

Oh, yeah. Rough was good.

Damn good.

The kiss went nuclear, and Teague found himself practically climbing Hudson's body, trying to get closer, *needing* to get closer. Teague reached between them, his hand circling both of their cocks, stroking easily, allowing his shaft to slide sinfully against Hudson's. How the man could make him go from zero to sixty in two seconds flat was beyond him, but no matter what, that was always the case. Teague didn't think he would ever get tired of this man.

Ever.

Hudson nipped Teague's bottom lip, which was one of the signs that he was ready to move on to something else. Hesitantly, Teague pulled back, meeting Hudson's hooded, dark gaze, the usual emerald green nearly the color of the forest at night.

When Hudson eased down to his knees, Teague put one hand on the man's shoulder to keep from falling over. He watched intently as Hudson took his cock in his mouth. Hell yes. Smooth, soft lips wrapped around his shaft, while the hot rasp of Hudson's tongue glided leisurely over him. Hudson didn't hurry, clearly back to the tormenting part of their evening.

"Fuck, yes," Teague moaned. "Love your mouth. Fucking love it."

He rocked his hips, pushing past Hudson's lips, trying to find a rhythm that wouldn't send him blasting off too soon. He was horny as fuck after Hudson's stunt that afternoon, but he didn't want to come too soon. He still wanted the man to fuck him.

Hudson dropped to his ass, then pulled Teague forward. They were close enough to the bed that Teague managed to keep from falling over by planting his palms on the mattress. He was now hovering over Hudson, pushing his cock past those sexy fucking lips that always knew how to drive him wild. Hudson's hands gripped his ass, pulling him forward, pushing him back, forcing Teague to fuck his mouth.

"Don't wanna come," he ground out through clenched teeth. "Not yet, Hudson. Fuck … not yet."

Hudson stopped instantly, the suction from his mouth disappearing.

Teague toppled onto the bed, remaining facedown.

He should've known what was coming, but once again, Hudson took him by surprise. The warmth of Hudson's breath grazed his asshole when Hudson gripped Teague's ass and forced his cheeks apart.

"Holy fuck…" Teague absolutely loved when Hudson ate his ass, and the man knew it. "Oh, fuck."

Teague fisted his hands in the comforter, pushing back when Hudson's tongue joined the mix, grinding his dick against the mattress, knowing if Hudson kept this up, he was going to come.

At this point, it was up to Hudson on how he wanted the rest of the evening to play out, because Teague was right there…

So close…

Of course, that would be the moment Hudson stopped.

Fucker.

HUDSON ABSOLUTELY LOVED PUSHING TEAGUE RIGHT TO the edge and then pulling him back. In the very beginning of their relationship, it hadn't gone over well with Teague. Over time, he seemed to have adjusted to it. Perhaps that was because Hudson knew Teague enjoyed the hell out of it, too, as long as he was going to get his in the end. Sure, Teague would probably curse a blue streak because of it—sometimes extremely loudly, sometimes not—but he would enjoy it, nonetheless.

But Hudson knew now was not the time to push Teague too far. This afternoon had been a total tease for Teague, and he only handled being forced to wait for a certain amount of time. Not to mention, Hudson was aching to slide into Teague's ass, be surrounded by him, consumed by him. It was an addiction he'd acquired some months ago, and the more time he spent with Teague, the more he craved him.

Grabbing the lubricant he had close at hand, Hudson quickly prepared himself, then stood behind Teague, who was partially hanging off the bed, his feet on the floor, facedown on the mattress.

Without finesse, Hudson guided his dick right where it was destined to be, sliding into the warmth of Teague's body, then leaning over him, cupping Teague's neck as he began pushing in deep, retreating slowly. He trailed his lips over Teague's shoulder, inhaling the intoxicating scent of the man.

"Oh, fuck… Love feeling you inside me." Teague's whispered moan went right to Hudson's heart.

Hudson covered him with his body, allowing Teague to bear his weight while he pumped his hips, brushing his lips over Teague's neck. How he longed to tell the man he loved him with words, but that would never happen, so he had to show him with his body.

"I know," Teague mumbled, as though he'd read Hudson's mind. "I love this, Hudson. I love you… Oh, God, yes… Take everything you need from me. You own me like no man ever will."

Hudson's heart constricted in his chest, emotion pouring through his veins. He loved Teague with an intensity that he still didn't understand. Having Teague's love in return was more than he'd ever imagined, more than he felt he deserved. But he'd take it. He'd take everything, because Teague wasn't the only one who was owned. Hudson belonged to Teague. Had since the very first time Hudson had kissed Teague back on a cruise ship the day their friends got married.

"Make me come," Teague pleaded. "Fuck me, Hudson. Show me how much you need me."

His blood thrummed through his veins, pounding in his head and his cock as that desperate need to possess Teague took over. He didn't retreat, didn't want to relinquish the heat of Teague's body. He continued to drive his cock deep into Teague's ass, thrusting harder, faster, driving them both where they needed to go.

"Oh, fuck … yes… Just like that. You're gonna make me come… I wanna feel you come in my ass… Hudson … oh, yeah … fuck, yeah…"

The kid definitely had a way with words.

Hudson gave Teague everything he had in him, slamming his hips forward, shaking the bed with the sheer intensity of his movements. Every moan, every rough inhale stoked the flames, made him burn hotter, desperate to take Teague right over the cliff with him.

"Fuck … oh, fuck… Hudson … I'm…"

Teague's muscles tensed, his ass strangling Hudson's dick as he came with a roar. Hudson didn't hold back, slamming into him again and again, needing more, needing everything. When the pressure became too much, he let himself go, pulsing inside Teague as he held on to him, praying like hell Teague knew exactly how much he meant to Hudson.

Teague's hand gripped Hudson's thigh, his short nails sliding over his skin.

"I love you."

Hudson moved his hand up near Teague's face and made the sign for I love you, so damn grateful that he'd found someone who understood and accepted him in every way.

Tuesday, December 13

"I HOPE LIKE HELL YOU AREN'T EXPECTING me to get up before the sun," Teague mumbled, feeling around on the bed for the warm body that was supposed to be next to him.

Ah, hell. He came up empty but still refused to open his eyes.

Instead, Teague rolled over onto his back, placing his arm over his face. He could hear Hudson across the hall, probably sorting all those damn Christmas ornaments so they could start putting them on the tree. After sex last night, Hudson had dragged Teague to the shower, then forced food down him before they finally gave in to sleep around midnight.

That was the way things were with them. Neither of them was on a schedule, except during the busy summer months when the boat repair shop was jumping. During the colder months, most people had their boats stored, only a few choosing to have major repairs completed so they'd be back in the water come May.

Right now, there was not much of anything for either of them to do. They helped with the upkeep at the marina, even volunteered for some of the events that took place on dry land. But for the most part, they spent endless amounts of time together simply being.

Teague loved every minute of it, too.

Except when it came to the stupid holidays. First Thanksgiving, now Christmas. Teague wasn't sure how he was going to make it through the rest of the year without losing his mind. The only reason he was coping was for Hudson's benefit.

The holidays and all the crap that came along with them were obviously important to Hudson; therefore, they were important to Teague, but not at five o'clock in the damn morning.

Charger jumped up onto the bed, clearly realizing that Teague was awake.

"Lemme guess," he grumbled as he dropped his arm and peered over at his dog. "You need to go out, and Hudson sent you to get me out of bed. You do realize it's still dark outside, right?"

The dog licked his face.

"Fantastic," he groaned, dropping his feet over the edge of the mattress and forcing himself to sit up. He ran his fingers through his hair, then glanced at the dog. "Me first, man."

Teague grabbed a pair of sweat pants, a T-shirt, and his shoes after using the restroom, then followed Charger out of the apartment and down the stairs. They made their way over to the trees near the water, and he waited patiently while Charger roamed around and did his business. The morning was cold, and Teague's nuts were threatening to shrivel up, but he didn't complain. Aside from Hudson, Charger was the best thing that had ever happened to him. The service dog had become his best friend these past few months, and he couldn't imagine his life without him. If that meant getting up at the butt crack of dawn so Charger could do what needed to be done, then so be it.

"You think Hudson's gonna ask a ton of questions when I tell him I need to run out to the store later?" Teague asked the dog, not expecting a response. "I've gotta get his Christmas present, and the store called to let me know it's ready."

It hadn't taken any thought at all for Teague to realize what he wanted to get the man for Christmas. He'd long ago accepted that he wanted to spend the rest of his life with Hudson, and asking the big guy to marry him was first and foremost on his to-do list. Truthfully, he wanted to do it before Hudson popped the question.

For whatever reason, it was important to Teague that he be the one to ask. He got the feeling that Hudson was going to give him all the time in the world to come to terms with their relationship. Truth was, he didn't need any more time. He was no longer second-guessing his feelings or his decisions. This was the life he wanted.

Charger nudged his thigh and Teague peered down at him.

"Thank God," he said, his breath crystallizing in the freezing air.

Five minutes later, they were back inside. He peeked into the living room to find Hudson putting the tree on the base and doing whatever had to be done for a live Christmas tree to survive until Christmas. Teague didn't have the first clue how any of that worked. He'd never shared a Christmas with anyone. Not that he could remember anyway.

"There's a first time for everything," he mumbled under his breath, watching Hudson work.

Teague couldn't help but smile.

He just couldn't.

HUDSON HAD WOKEN UP EARLY, AS HE usually did. Rather than stay in his warm bed, curled up with Teague, he'd opted to get up and start getting the tree ready. Clearly he hadn't been as quiet as he'd hoped, because Teague had wandered in a minute ago with the dog close to his side.

Peering back at him over his shoulder, Hudson smiled.

"I'm not helping," Teague noted. "But I don't mind watching. Especially since you refuse to put a shirt on."

Hudson grinned, turning back to the tree. It was as good as it was going to get, and it was now ready for lights and ornaments. He was tempted to turn decorating the damn thing into a sexual game with Teague. The kid never could resist when it came to sex. He was as insatiable as Hudson, which made them the perfect pair.

Getting to his feet, Hudson moved over to the boxes that he'd placed on the couch. He looked up at Teague and signed: *Refusing to help?*

"Damn straight I am. I'd rather use my energy on downing some Cheerios while you take care of that shit."

Hudson detected a hint of amusement in Teague's tone. He knew the man did that on purpose, constantly needling him into doing what he wanted. Hudson couldn't deny giving in to him, either. Hell, it was entertaining, to say the least. Not to mention hot.

He grabbed a string of lights and moved back to the tree. He felt Teague's eyes on him as he went to work. It took a solid ten minutes before he had the light strands hanging the way he wanted them. When he finished, he took a step back to look. Teague came to stand beside him, bowl of cereal in one hand.

"I'm gonna have to run out for a little while this afternoon," Teague informed him, grabbing an ornament and handing it over.

Want me to come along?

"Not this time, no. I've got to … uh … pick something up."

My Christmas present?

"No," Teague said with a snort. "What makes you think I'm getting you a present?"

He could tell by Teague's tone that he was messing with him.

I say no presents this year.

"I couldn't agree more. Less hassle and no one has to worry about being disappointed by opening socks or underwear. What if we just trade sexual favors?"

Right. One thing Teague wasn't good at … lying. It was clear that whatever his plans were did involve a present. Not that Hudson wanted Teague to get him anything. As far as he was concerned, he had absolutely everything he could ever want. Having Teague in his life, sleeping in his bed, waking up by his side in the morning … that was enough. He didn't need anything more than that.

Sexual favors are good.

"Of course they are." Teague handed him another ornament. "Especially when they come from me."

Hudson placed the ornament on the tree.

Remember, we agreed to go to AJ's for dinner.

"Shit," Teague grumbled, but the tone didn't match the humor dancing in his eyes. "Is the pregnant girl gonna be there?"

Hudson grinned. *Yes, Milly will be there.*

Since the day Milly had informed Hudson's brother, AJ, that she was pregnant—an accident that had taken place on the cruise back in May—the two of them had been spending quite a bit of time together. Now that she was six months along, he wasn't sure which one was freaking out more. They were getting quite antsy. Neither of them seemed to know what was going on. If Hudson didn't know better, he'd say they were both clueless over how this was going to work out. However, they would probably figure it out right quick once the baby was born.

Cam and Gannon will be there.

Teague frowned. "Seriously?"

Hudson nodded.

"Great."

It was no secret that, at one point, Teague had had a hard time when it came to big gatherings. Hudson knew he didn't enjoy getting that close to people, but he was getting better. He figured now wasn't the time to inform Teague that they were planning a huge Christmas dinner with everyone. Cam and Gannon, Cam's dad, Dare and Noah, Dare's grandmother, Roan, as well as Milly and AJ. It was going to be interesting, to say the least. The plan had come together one day when Teague had been out and Hudson asked if they could keep it on the down low until he had the chance to talk to Teague about it. If Teague refused to go, Hudson wasn't going to force him or try to guilt-trip him, either.

"You hungry?" Teague asked, obviously trying to change the subject.

Hudson nodded.

"I'll make breakfast while you"—Teague waved his hand toward the tree—"do whatever it is you're doin' to that thing. Cheerios or Cap'n Crunch?"

Eggs and bacon.

Teague looked at him as though he'd lost his mind.

Hudson waited patiently.

"Fine. Two eggs?"

He offered another nod, keeping his eyes trained on Teague as he sauntered out of the apartment and across the hall. When Teague was out of sight, Hudson turned toward the tree once more.

He knew Teague was putting on a good show. They'd talked at length about their pasts. About how Teague's mother had committed suicide when he was a very small boy, about how he'd grown up in one foster home after another, never getting attached. Hudson had grown up with his mother and his brother, AJ. Their mother had succumbed to depression and taken her own life when Hudson was a teenager, and by then, AJ had been old enough to ensure Hudson wasn't pulled into the system. Needless to say, they had a lot in common, but significant differences as well.

Hudson wanted nothing more than to create his own family traditions with Teague. He wanted to show the man he loved that the things he spent his life running from were no longer a threat to him. Hudson was there to catch him if he fell and vice versa.

And this Christmas was the first of many to come for the two of them.

Yeah. It was safe to say there were no gifts necessary this year. Hudson had every damn thing he could ever want. But that didn't mean they wouldn't be exchanged.

No way was Hudson spending his first Christmas with Teague and not trying to give him everything he wanted.

And then some.

CHAPTER 5

"Let me see," Milly insisted, her voice low.

Teague peered around the room to ensure Hudson wasn't hiding in some dark corner watching him right that very moment. When he realized the coast was clear, he pulled the jewelry box out of his pocket and flipped it open.

Milly drew in a deep breath, her eyes turning glassy when she looked up at him.

"Oh, Teague. You did good. They're … perfect."

Yeah, he had to admit, he'd done pretty well in picking them out. The matching black stainless bands weren't anything fancy, but considering neither of them ever wore jewelry of any type, Teague figured they were perfect for them.

Milly pulled them out of the box and stared at them, twisting and turning as she read the inscription on the inside of each: *Forever and a day.* Teague would admit he wasn't the most poetic, but he'd wanted something. So, he'd gone with that.

He frowned when he realized Milly was crying.

Laughing, she waved him off, tucking the rings back where they belonged. "Pregnancy hormones. This morning, I cried because I missed one washcloth when I started a load of laundry. You'da thought it was the end of the world."

Teague chuckled.

"Seriously, though, I love them. Hudson's one lucky guy."

Teague knew it was the reverse, but he didn't bother to tell Milly that.

"When are you gonna propose?" she whispered, her eyes scanning their surroundings.

"Christmas morning," he told her. "That day seems to mean something to him, and this way, it'll mean something to both of us."

Milly was studying his face, her smile gentle. "I'm happy for both of you, Teague. And I'm grateful to have you both in my life."

Sentimental Milly was relatively new. The woman was usually witty and sarcastic, but the pregnancy was bringing out a softer side to her. Oh, sure, she still had a crazy comeback for everything, but this side of her seemed to be dominating these days.

Not knowing what to say, he mumbled, "Ditto."

Teague tucked the box back into his pocket when AJ and Hudson appeared in the kitchen. AJ moved directly to Milly's side, watching her closely.

"You okay?"

She nodded, beaming up at him.

Teague was fascinated by the pair. He wasn't even sure why that was. When he first learned that they were pregnant, Teague had wondered what that would mean for them. They seemed to be working things out. He wasn't quite sure the status of their relationship, but it was obvious they were both in support of the baby. Personally, he wasn't fond of surprises, so he couldn't imagine what they were going through.

"Anyone ready for dessert?"

Teague cast a glance at Hudson, grinning sheepishly. He doubted AJ was referring to what he had in mind, but he definitely wasn't above planting that little seed in Hudson's brain.

The look he got back was exactly what he'd expected. Hudson didn't take kindly to being teased. Not that Teague would stop anytime soon. If the man continued to insist Teague be a part of these little get-togethers, he was going to insist on getting something out of the deal.

Hudson moved to stand behind him, his hand resting on Teague's hip. He liked that the man didn't shy away from him in public. It wasn't that Teague wanted to be the center of attention—which tended to happen when a couple of the same sex were intimate in public—but he would rather deal with that as long as it meant Hudson remained close.

"I'm always up for dessert," Milly said, smiling at Teague. When Hudson and AJ turned away, she mouthed, "You did well," then disappeared.

Funny, now that he had the rings, Teague was eager to pop the question. Waiting until Christmas was going to be a serious test of his patience. Twelve days were a long time.

He didn't think too hard on the fact that his patience had never been all that strong to begin with.

HUDSON COULDN'T WAIT TO GET TEAGUE HOME. The kid knew exactly what to do to get under Hudson's skin. A slight brush against him here, a wicked, needy look there... Hudson was ready to drag the man to the bathroom and fuck him senseless just for being so damn sexy.

And he would have if getting him home and making him fly apart in a million different directions wasn't more important. Oh, and of course, he needed a little privacy to make that happen.

"You've got that look in your eye, big guy," Teague said with a knowing smirk. "I'm gettin' lucky tonight, aren't I?"

Hudson narrowed his eyes and then pointed toward the door.

"Headin' out?" AJ inquired as he joined them in the living room.

"Looks like it," Teague answered. "You know me, I'm all for hangin' out with friends for the rest of the night, but Hudson's a bit of a recluse. Likes his privacy. Looks like I need to get him home."

Everyone laughed, as Teague obviously meant them to.

"Well, thanks for coming," AJ told them both. "Christmas is less than two weeks away. We'll see you then, right?"

"With bells on," Teague noted with a hint of sarcasm.

Hudson inwardly grinned. Three months ago, Teague would've been waiting by the front door, not talking to anyone. At least now he added his brilliant sarcasm to the mix.

Hudson signed: *We will be there. What do you need us to bring?*

"Whatever you want," AJ said. "We're supplying the turkey and all the fixings. If your boy here makes a mean pecan pie, he's welcome to bring it."

"Pecan pie," Teague muttered, staring at the ground.

Hudson wrapped his arm around Teague and pulled him into him, nodding at AJ as he did. Before anyone could detain them longer, Hudson led Teague out the door and over to the truck.

Fifteen minutes later, they were pulling into the parking lot of the marina. Surprisingly, Teague didn't bolt from the truck. He was rather civil, getting out slowly, opening the door for Charger. That was a new development for Teague as well. Previously, after spending the evening with their friends, the man would run for peace and quiet as soon as the opportunity presented itself.

Teague really was a different man than he'd been months ago.

Hudson led the way up the stairs, then unlocked the door and stepped back so they could go inside. He allowed Teague to make it ten feet before he was on him, pushing him against the wall, pressing up against his back. The man groaned, a delicious sound that told Hudson he was all for playing this game right now.

"It's good, Charger," Teague whispered when the dog turned around to stare at them. "So fucking good. Go lie down."

Charger turned and wandered into the living room, probably to find his spot on the couch. Hudson nipped Teague's ear, running both hands around to his chest, clutching his shirt as he lowered his head and kissed Teague's ear. Unable to resist kissing him, Hudson freed one of his hands and gripped Teague's hair, pulling his head back so he'd have access to Teague's mouth.

Another moan from Teague. "God, yes. Do you even know how much I need this? You dominating me?"

Hudson kissed him again, loving that Teague was open when it came to how he felt.

"I fucking crave it, Hudson."

Hudson yanked at the button on Teague's jeans, continuing to press his chest against Teague's back, pushing him into the wall. He wasn't gentle when he freed Teague's cock, gripping it tightly, stroking him roughly while Teague jerked his hips and fucked Hudson's hand.

"Harder," Teague pleaded.

Hudson tightened his grip, grinding his cock against Teague's ass. He wanted to take him right here in the hallway. Unfortunately, he hadn't thought it all the way through, and the lube was in the bedroom.

"Pocket," Teague groaned. "Check my pocket."

Hudson released Teague's cock and reached for Teague's pocket.

"No! The other one."

Pulling back slowly, he changed hands and shoved his hand in Teague's other pocket, coming out with a small packet of lube. He should've known.

Without hesitation, he shoved Teague's jeans down to his knees, then freed himself. Within a minute, he had his dick lubed and was pushing into Teague from behind.

Teague slammed his palms against the wall, thrusting his hips back against Hudson.

"Fuck me… Oh, God, yes, Hudson. Love this."

They both did. There were times Hudson thought he would fucking explode for wanting this man. His body could hardly contain the ridiculous urges the kid instilled in him. He'd long ago stopped worrying that he would hurt Teague. They both wanted it, needed it. Craved it.

Hudson dug his fingers into Teague's hips, jerking him back as he slammed into him over and over, taking what he wanted from the man.

"Don't stop…" Teague's warning was given on a shaky breath.

Hudson didn't stop. He continued to thrust his hips forward, back, forward, back. He drove as deep into Teague's ass as he could. Leaning forward, he nipped Teague's neck, sucking his skin into his mouth, savoring the taste of him, spurred on by Teague's cries of pleasure.

He didn't know how long they were there, how many minutes had passed before his release surged upon him. Needing Teague to come first, Hudson reached around and grabbed Teague's swollen cock, jerking him roughly, making him beg for more.

Hudson refused to come until Teague did, but he was dangerously close.

"Aww … fuck yes… Come for me, Hudson. Right. Fucking. Now."

Sensory overload made him see spots as he slammed into Teague one final time, coming hard as Teague's dick jerked and pulsed in his hand.

And then it was over. He could hardly hold himself up. Teague took his weight as Hudson leaned into him, kissing Teague's neck, trying to get his heart to stop slamming against his ribs.

When they were both steady on their feet, Hudson withdrew, then turned toward the bedroom, taking Teague's hand and dragging him with him.

"That right there…" Teague said from behind him. "That's what I want for Christmas. All day."

Hudson grinned.

The kid was going to be the death of him.

CHAPTER 6

Thursday, December 22

"I CAN'T WAIT ANY LONGER, CHARGER," TEAGUE mumbled as he paced the hallway between the two apartments.

Hudson was at the repair shop taking care of something, and Teague was going out of his mind. His patience had long ago run thin, and he knew he was going to break any minute now.

"I'm ready," he told the dog. "I need to get this over with."

Charger sat near the door, staring back at him. The little guy probably thought Teague was talking about going outside.

Nope.

In fact, he was tempted to head right down to the shop and drop to one knee and get this whole proposal thing over with. He was becoming a nervous wreck.

"I'm not good at this shit," he continued, pivoting on his heel and heading back the way he'd come. "What if Hudson doesn't want to get married? What if he says no? Or worse … what if he laughs at me?"

Teague knew his insecurities were getting the best of him, but he couldn't help it. Ever since he'd picked up the rings, they'd been on his mind. He wanted to get this over with before he lost his nerve. But he wanted it to be special for Hudson. He didn't want to blow the whole damn thing. Although knowing him, he would anyway.

Teague's phone buzzed in his pocket. He jolted to a stop and pulled it out.

Come down to the repair shop.

He smiled at himself. The cocky man had no problems telling him what to do.

Can't.

Smiling, he resumed his pacing, waiting for Hudson to respond.

I wasn't asking.

No, he wasn't. And the demand was sexy as fuck, making Teague's dick jerk to attention. But even the thought of sex in the middle of the afternoon wasn't enough to calm his nerves.

Teague responded with: *Maybe you should try asking sometime. Might get you somewhere.*

He knew Hudson would only tolerate so much before he showed up at the apartment and took whatever it was he wanted. Teague happened to love that shit. The fact that his man couldn't seem to keep his hands off him … complete and total turn-on.

Sometimes it was still hard for Teague to believe that Hudson was his. After all the shit he'd been through in his life, for things to go from bleak to bright seemed crazy. Yet here he was, living a life he'd never imagined, feeling things he'd never thought possible.

One more time. Come down to the shop.

Teague smiled as he read the text. Looked as though he wasn't going to get out of this one.

Fine.

With a huff, Teague tucked his phone in his pocket, put the rings back where he'd had them stashed in the apartment, then headed outside with Charger in tow. Ten minutes later, after Charger sniffed around for a while, Teague wandered into the boat shop. The bay door was closed, so he went to the other door and let himself in. He found Hudson standing there, arms crossed over his massive chest, eyes locked on him.

Hudson's hands fell and he signed for Teague to lock the door.

"Still not hearing please," he muttered aloud, locking the door behind him.

As usual, Charger made a beeline for the bed they had in the shop.

Hudson crooked his finger, urging Teague to come to him.

Teague wanted to resist. It was what he did. Only he knew it never worked. No matter how hard he tried, he always gave in to Hudson. It was what he lived for.

He walked slowly, sliding his hand over the toolbox as he moved closer, never taking his eyes off the big guy. Hudson shifted, leaning his ass against one of the lower toolboxes as Teague approached. When he was within reach, Teague found himself being jerked forward, crashing into Hudson.

It was then that Hudson kissed him.

He fought the urge to sigh with contentment, but he gave in nonetheless. No way could he resist kissing this man. For the longest time, that was the only thing Hudson did. With the smell of oil permeating the air, Teague let himself get caught up in Hudson's arms, holding on to him for dear life.

Yeah. This was the life he lived. And he was starting to realize it wasn't too good to be true.

Although there was the possibility that the act of simply kissing this man could turn into something wicked in an instant, that hadn't been Hudson's reason for summoning Teague down here.

Hudson had merely wanted to see him. To kiss him. To touch him.

He wasn't sure why he always had the urge to be around him, but he did. Always. When they were apart, Hudson felt as though part of himself was missing, and he loved spending time with Teague. Watching television, having dinner, sitting on the dock. Those were the times he enjoyed most.

"Is that why you told me to come down here?" Teague mumbled, pulling back slightly. "To kiss the daylights out of me?"

Hudson shrugged, smiled.

"I like when you do shit like that."

Hudson pulled him in again, pressing his lips to Teague's. He didn't go for domination. That was for later. Right now, he wanted to taste, to touch, to inhale this man.

When he finally pulled back, Teague grinned up at him. "I think we should take the rest of the week off."

Hudson cocked an eyebrow and waited.

"It's almost Christmas. No one gives a shit about their boat right now. Let's take the days off, get naked, and stay that way through the weekend."

Hudson liked that plan. Except they would be going to Cam and Gannon's for dinner on Sunday. They'd already committed to going, and Hudson wasn't about to go back on that. However, that didn't mean they couldn't stay holed up until then.

That was, if Teague could last that long. The kid didn't do well when he was cooped up for long periods. They both knew that.

"I'll make it worth your while," Teague whispered, his hand sliding down Hudson's chest, moving closer and closer to Hudson's iron-hard cock.

He waited, knowing Teague was going to do his best to convince him. Hudson didn't need to tell him that he'd already made up his mind.

After all, where was the fun in that?

As he'd assumed it would, Teague's hand dropped to the button on Hudson's jeans. He waited patiently, trying to keep his breathing under control. When the button popped free and the zipper slid down, Hudson dropped his gaze to Teague's hand, watching as he slowly freed him from the confining denim.

"I know you want to feel my mouth on you."

Hudson lifted his head, met Teague's taunting gaze. He didn't give himself away, though.

"Yeah. That's what you want," Teague whispered. "You want me to wrap my lips around your dick, to suck you deep into my mouth."

Okay, clearly the kid was pushing him on purpose. Hudson had a tremendous amount of willpower, except when it came to Teague. It was hard enough to keep his hands off the man when they were working. And when they weren't...

"Watch me, Hudson," Teague instructed. "Don't take your eyes off me while I suck your dick."

His breath caught in his lungs, trapped as his body hardened, his cock pulsing with the promises he could see in Teague's blue eyes.

Teague slowly dropped to his knees, his fingers circling Hudson's dick, teasing him with the lightest of touches. As Teague wanted, Hudson never looked away. He watched as Teague leaned closer, his warm breath caressing the swollen head, causing pre-cum to form on the tip.

His eyes widened, his stomach muscles contracting when Teague's tongue darted out, lightly stroking the head, lapping up the bead of liquid pooled there. The kid was brutal with his torment. He never hurried and Hudson didn't rush him. He gripped the toolbox he was perched against, allowing Teague to have total control over him.

Hudson had to admit, allowing Teague control over him was an overwhelming experience. Every time he allowed it, he seemed to crave it more. He wanted to put himself in Teague's hands, to allow the man his deepest, darkest desires. He couldn't stop thinking about it anymore.

"You like that?" Teague asked, licking him like a lollipop while staring up at him.

Hudson nodded. He fucking loved it.

"What about this?"

Teague opened his mouth wider and enveloped Hudson's cock in the warm cavern of his mouth, sliding all the way down on him. Hudson sucked in air, the head of his cock brushing Teague's tonsils. Fucking hell, that was incredible. His fingers tightened on the edge of the toolbox.

Teague continued to suck him deeper while tugging Hudson's jeans down his thighs. He had no idea what the kid had in store for him, but he waited, focusing on breathing while the pleasure obliterated his brain cells.

Hudson continued to watch, noticing when Teague pulled back, dipping his middle finger into his mouth.

"Spread your legs as far as you can," Teague instructed.

Hudson did, but it wasn't an easy feat when he was shackled by his jeans.

Teague's mouth returned to his cock, engulfing him while his finger slid between Hudson's ass cheeks, finding his asshole. Gently, Teague pushed the tip inside, retreated. He choreographed his movements, fucking Hudson's ass with his finger while bobbing up and down on his cock.

It was too much.

Hudson had thought he'd be the one in control when he summoned Teague down here, but that clearly wasn't the case.

Unable to stop himself, Hudson released the toolbox and grabbed Teague's head, fisting his hair roughly as he pulled him onto his dick just as he came so hard he saw stars.

Heaven help him.

CHAPTER 7

Friday, December 23

TEAGUE MADE AS MUCH NOISE AS POSSIBLE while he prepared dinner. He knew Hudson was trying to watch television, and it amused him to irritate the man.

Yes, it had been Teague's idea to stay home, but admittedly, he had cabin fever. The few times he'd taken Charger outside, spending at least an hour each time, did nothing to alleviate the frustration growing in him. He needed to do something, but he didn't know what. It wasn't that he wanted to go somewhere, but he was bored.

Hudson's head turned and he pinned Teague with a look.

"What?" he questioned, smiling. "If you want peace and quiet, *you* cook."

Hudson looked amused, but he didn't move from his spot on the couch.

Clearly Teague was going to have to work harder.

Ten minutes later, Teague got his wish. Hudson was up off the couch, storming into the small kitchen, a murderous gleam in his eyes.

Of course, Teague laughed, which was obviously not what the big guy wanted.

Within seconds, Teague found himself naked as the day he was born, his clothes somewhere in the living room, while Hudson stood behind him, watching him finish preparing their dinner.

"You always like to see me naked," he groused, trying not to smile. "Not sure why I have to cook in the nude. Good thing there's no grease or you might be shit out of luck for a few days."

Hudson didn't move.

"What happens if I burn my dick? You gonna kiss it and make it better?" Teague asked as he pulled the glass pan out of the oven. The chicken he'd been baking was done. "Or better yet, what if I scorch my ass? This pan is hot, you know? You gonna kiss my ass if that happens?"

He peered over his shoulder to see Hudson staring at his ass. His dick definitely liked that he was. He had to will the damn thing to stay down. He might tease about getting burned, but he damn sure wasn't interested in it actually happening.

As he plated the asparagus and chicken, he felt the warmth of Hudson's body behind him. Seconds later, Hudson's hands were on his ass, cupping his cheeks, squeezing.

Teague inhaled sharply.

Okay, tempting the beast wasn't always a good thing. Especially when Teague knew Hudson wasn't going to follow through. At least not until after dinner.

One big hand slid between his thighs, cupping his nuts. Teague nearly dropped the plate he was holding. He set it down abruptly, leaning into Hudson while the big man fondled his balls.

"Fuck," he groaned. "Oh, fuck, Hudson."

The hand disappeared all too soon.

"You're a fucking tease," he muttered, knowing he was the one who'd asked for this. "Just for that, I'm not giving it up tonight. How's that make you feel?"

The look Hudson shot him said he didn't buy it for a second.

"I'm serious," he continued. "Just watch. You'll be jacking off while I'm asleep."

Hudson grinned, then joined Teague at the table. Teague managed to keep his mouth shut long enough for them to eat. He was trying to come up with another way to harass the man, but hadn't actually gotten far into a plan when Hudson stood from his chair, took the plates, then dumped them in the sink.

"Hey. What if I wasn't finished?"

He was finished.

Hudson cocked his eyebrow in that sexy way that made Teague's dick twitch. The damn thing didn't have a stitch covering it, so now wasn't the time for twitching.

Hudson signed: *Get up.*

Teague shook his head.

Want me to make you?

Teague nodded. Then laughed.

Of course, that wasn't the right thing to do, because Hudson was on him in a second, pulling him out of the chair, then practically dragging him across the hall to their bedroom. Teague couldn't keep his feet under him when Hudson pushed him onto the mattress, then climbed over him, straddling his thighs.

"Sorry, big guy," he said, trying to sound as though he really was. "I've got a headache. All that cooking naked. It really pushes my limits."

I will push your limits.

"Maybe tomorrow, but thanks for the offer." Teague never took his eyes off Hudson.

The next thing he knew, Hudson had flipped him over onto his stomach, once again straddling his legs, holding him down. Warm breath fanned his face as Hudson ground his jean-clad cock against Teague's ass. What he wouldn't give for the man to be naked right now. He loved when Hudson got all demanding with him.

"Good night," Teague snapped, closing his eyes and pretending to sleep.

The hand that landed on his ass made him jump.

"Shit! What the hell was that?"

One big palm landed in the middle of his back, effectively holding him down while Hudson spanked him again.

Fuck. That shit should not feel good, but damn it to hell. It did. Teague's dick was doing a happy dance, crushed between him and the mattress. He'd never pushed Hudson this far, but hell. He made a mental note of what he did, because if he were lucky, he would have a chance to do it again.

HONESTLY, HUDSON HADN'T INTENDED TO TAKE THINGS this far, but the fact that Teague was groaning, his ass lifting as Hudson smacked him with an open palm again and again, told him he liked it.

The kid was going to be the death of him.

He'd known that Teague was battling with being cooped up for so long. It had been evident in everything he did throughout the day. And that was the very reason Hudson had stripped him naked. He'd wanted to take Teague's mind off of it.

Apparently, that had worked.

"Fuck…" Teague cried out. "I'm not sure I'm supposed to fucking like that, but goddamn … Hudson…"

Yeah. Hudson knew just what he meant. As it was, he was about to bust his fucking zipper. Glancing down, he saw the slightly reddened skin of Teague's ass, and his body jerked. He was so fucking hard he hurt.

Leaning down, he nipped Teague's shoulder, continuing to grind himself against Teague's ass.

Wanting to make this last for Teague, Hudson finally pulled himself away. He got to his feet, then quickly shed his clothes before coming to stand beside the bed, close to Teague's head. He slid his fingers into the cool blond strands, forcefully tugging until Teague moved closer to the edge of the bed. When he was within reach, Hudson fed his cock into Teague's mouth.

Damn.

He sucked air into his lungs as he pumped his hips, fucking Teague's mouth, taking what the man was offering. He wasn't gentle, but he knew Teague didn't need him to be. If it weren't for the fact he fully intended to fuck Teague into oblivion, he would've come right down Teague's throat. Instead, he gritted his teeth and continued to stave off the incredible need to come while he was overwhelmed by sensations.

When he finally had no choice but to pull back, Teague frowned up at him. He shook his head, knowing the man would give him a hard time as long as they were both walking this earth. It was what Teague did. Not that Hudson minded. He loved him for it. That was why they worked.

Grabbing the lube from the nightstand, Hudson moved around to the other side of the bed. He slicked his cock, dribbled more lube on Teague's ass, then easily slid home. And that's the moment he reached down deep for his patience, taking it slow, driving Teague absolutely crazy.

"You're a bastard," Teague grumbled. "Fuck me, damn you. Fuck me like you mean it."

Hudson continued to slide in deep, then retreat. By the time he was so consumed by the blinding pressure for release, Hudson was sweating and Teague was still cursing.

Gripping Teague's hips, Hudson jerked him up onto his knees, pulling him with him as he got off the bed. With his feet on the floor, his fingers digging into Teague's hips, he began pounding him hard and fast. The bed jerked and creaked with every movement while Teague cried out, begging for more.

It was brutal and beautiful, and Hudson never wanted it to end. He didn't let up for long minutes, his thigh muscles screaming by the time he could take no more.

"Fuck! Fuck, fuck, fuck!" Teague slammed back against him. "Oh, yeah!"

As Teague came, his body jerking against Hudson's hold, he didn't let up, thrusting into him again and again until his body was no longer his own. He came so hard he nearly passed out, driving deep into Teague's ass as he fell over the man, his lungs burning for oxygen.

"I'm pretty sure you misunderstood me," Teague said, his breaths as labored as Hudson's. "When I said I had a headache, it meant I *didn't* want sex."

The kid made him absolutely crazy.

And he loved him even more now than ever before.

CHAPTER 8

Saturday, December 24

FROM THE MOMENT HIS EYES OPENED THIS morning, Teague had felt the tremors in his hands. Nerves. That was all it was, but still. He was having a damn hard time focusing, and it was no one's fault but his. With the rings in his pocket, he was doubly nervous. What if Hudson found them? What if the big guy ruined Teague's surprise?

And yes, Teague was supposed to wait until tomorrow to pop the question, but he'd had all he could stand with this waiting bullshit. He would be doing this today.

Now that the day was nearly half over, Teague was still wondering why he hadn't simply gotten on with it yet. He could've easily popped the question half a dozen times, but he wanted the moment to be perfect.

Perfection did not involve Teague making cereal for breakfast or grilled cheese for lunch. It did not involve Hudson sitting in front of the television. And it certainly didn't involve following Charger halfway around the marina. Twice.

Wait.

Maybe that was the key.

Maybe Teague needed to get Hudson down by the water. That made perfect sense, right? It was a place they both loved, where they had ultimately met. Okay, Teague liked where his brain was going with this.

He glanced over at Charger. The dog was curled up on the couch, clearly content to be doing absolutely nothing on Christmas Eve, while Teague felt as though he was going to go insane.

Something must've clued Hudson in to Teague's mood, because the man looked over at him, a question on his face.

"I'm goin' for a walk," he blurted, turning for the door. "Come on, Charger."

The dog was instantly at his side, tail wagging, tongue lolling. Yep, they were going to do this.

When Hudson didn't follow immediately, Teague made sure to slam the door, hoping the guy would catch on. That or he'd think Teague was throwing a hissy fit and leave him to his own devices.

And wouldn't that just backfire right in Teague's face.

Taking a deep breath, Teague headed down the stairs, around the building, then toward the water. Charger took his time, checking everything out while Teague snuck backward glances at the office.

No Hudson.

He wondered how long he would have to stay out there before he got the big guy's attention. Ten minutes? Thirty? An hour?

Jesus Christ.

Today was going to be a really long day.

Teague opted not to think about it, choosing to walk around, following the dog, trying to be patient. Hudson would follow, of that he had no doubt. Granted, Teague would have to wait him out, but that was okay. What else did he have to do today? As it was, he had his thumb up his butt. Well, not literally. Yet.

Thankfully, it only took half an hour before Hudson wandered down from upstairs. He'd pulled on a pair of sweat pants and a hoodie rather than the shorts and T-shirt he had been wearing. The wind had a bite to it, but it wasn't too bad. Teague's fingers had gone numb long ago, but other than that, he was all right.

He turned to watch Hudson walking toward them, shuffling closer to the water with every step. Teague stood there, not moving. Hell, he was hardly breathing. He had to shove his hands into his pockets to keep the damn things from giving away his nerves.

Hudson signed: *Problem?*

Teague smiled. "Define problem."

Hudson frowned, studying him intently.

Knowing it was now or never, Teague eliminated the distance between them, grabbing Hudson's hand and pulling him closer.

"I need to talk to you about something."

Clearly Hudson wasn't happy about that based on the expression that contorted his handsome features. Perhaps it was the way Teague had said it. They both knew Teague wasn't big on talking about his feelings, so he could see why Hudson would be concerned.

Swallowing hard, he relaxed his grip on Hudson's hand and stared up into the man's face. This incredible man whom he loved with everything that he was.

Because he was holding Hudson's hands, the man couldn't sign, which was good. Teague needed a minute, but not too long. As it was, he'd been stewing for days now, which made him jumpy and nervous and...

"Okay ... so..." Good God, he felt like he was going to throw up. He inhaled deeply, let it out slowly.

Hudson's fingers closed over Teague's, his grip tightening.

"I'm good," he assured Hudson. "I swear it."

Hudson nodded.

"I need to say something. So don't interrupt me, okay?"

Teague ignored the sexy way Hudson's eyebrow lifted, a clear challenge. If the man didn't like what Teague had to say, he would definitely interrupt. And he didn't need to be able to verbalize anything, because he had his own way of stopping the conversation when he wanted to.

Teague took another step toward Hudson, keeping their fingers linked as he wrapped his arms around Hudson, effectively pinning Hudson's hands behind his back.

"I love you," Teague said, his tone serious for possibly the first time in his life. "I don't think that's news to you. At least, I hope it's not. I'm not sure I'm the greatest at expressing my feelings, but I'd like to think you know me well enough to know what's in my heart." Teague glanced away. "God, this is harder than I thought."

Hudson tugged his hands from Teague's, then curled his finger beneath Teague's chin, forcing him to look at the man.

He took one more deep breath and decided it was now or never.

HUDSON TRIED TO HIDE THE WORRY THAT was churning in his gut. He hadn't seen Teague this worked up in a really long time. Now that he thought about it, the kid had been acting strange for the past few days, but Hudson had chalked that up to cabin fever. Teague didn't do well when he was confined to small spaces for long periods of time.

"I'm not the romantic type," Teague continued. "I don't care about roses and candlelight, but I don't think you do either. Shit." Teague's eyes widened. "Do you? Care about that shit? Should I be bringing you roses? Damn it."

Teague's eyes implored him, but Hudson remained completely still. Teague would get where he was going eventually; Hudson knew that much.

"Okay, fine. Whatever. That's not important. Well, it is, but it isn't. Not right now anyway." Teague drew a deep breath in, then continued, "If you do need roses and candlelight, I'll make that happen. Because I love you. I want to make you happy. I believe in you and me. I've spent my entire life isolated, alone, and I'm definitely not good at this shit, but I'm trying. I've never wanted anyone in my life because I didn't want to risk losing them. Until you. As cliché as it sounds, you complete me, big guy. You add color to my world, sometimes too much. I get overwhelmed by it, but you seem to get that, too."

Hudson's heart squeezed in his chest. He could hear the sincerity in Teague's tone, see the love shining in his eyes.

"Hudson…" Teague swallowed hard. "I want to spend the rest of my life with you. Not just today or tomorrow or even next week. Forever. And plenty of days after that."

Teague's hand moved, sliding into his pocket, and Hudson watched curiously, waiting to see where this was going. Before he could process it entirely, Teague dropped to one knee in front of him.

It took everything in him not to follow him to the ground. His heart was pounding like a bass drum, and he could hear the roar of his blood in his ears.

Teague opened a small velvet box, then held it open, lifting it so Hudson could see.

There were two rings in the box, a matching set. His heart turned over because it didn't take a rocket scientist to figure out what this was all about.

"I didn't buy you anything for Christmas, Hudson," Teague admitted, his eyes glassy. "I'm not good at that. I don't even know what to buy you, but I did buy these. For us … because I want to…" Teague choked on his words, but he didn't look away. "I want to marry you. I want to spend the rest of my life with you. I want to wake up every single day with you beside me. I'm not perfect, and I know that. I know there are things about me that you'd like to change. Hell, I'd like to change them, too. Just so I can make you happy."

Hudson couldn't stop the tears that leaked from his eyes. He couldn't remember the last time that he'd cried, but Teague was breaking his heart right here.

When Teague clearly wasn't going to continue, Hudson held up his hands so he could sign a response. He noticed his hands were trembling, but he went for it anyway.

First of all, the answer is yes. Second, there is absolutely nothing about you that I want to change. Nothing. And I want you to understand that above all else. I love you. Just as you are. Hudson went to his knee in front of Teague. *Only you. And I love the real you. The damaged, broken man who loves me with all that he is.*

He noticed Teague was crying, too, although he was desperately trying not to, and Hudson knew that had to be killing the kid. Teague did not like to show emotion, but it was obvious it had boiled up inside him and was begging for release.

I have known nothing better than spending my days with you. Loving you. Seeing you smile, laugh. Even watching you pout. Teague grinned sheepishly, so Hudson continued. *I love you just as you are.*

"So you'll marry me? Let me take your name?"

Hudson thought for a moment he would fall over. To keep himself from doing so, he grabbed Teague, slamming his lips over Teague's while the emotion won, filling him to overflowing.

"I take that as a yes? I can take your name?" Teague laughed on a sob when they pulled apart.

Definitely yes.

"Oh, thank God," Teague blurted. "I thought I was going to lose my mind just waiting for this moment. I'm not a patient man."

No kidding.

"But I did it," Teague said with pride. "I waited, I asked…"

And I said yes.

"So when's the wedding? I don't want anything elaborate," Teague rambled. "I mean it, Hudson. I'm all for going to dinner with the people we know, but I don't want anyone at my wedding. I want to get it over with. The two of us. That's it. And whoever officiates it. Nothing elaborate. No fancy bullshit. You. Me. Vows. Then I get to be Teague Ballard."

Teague Ballard. God, Hudson would love to give his name to this man. He'd never thought marriage was in his future, didn't think he'd find someone who would make him feel complete.

Hudson nodded. *Just you and me. Got it.*

And he did. Teague had come so far in the months since Hudson had initiated his challenge to the kid. Hudson would give Teague the world if he could. And he would not fight him on this. There would be plenty of battles to choose from during the long life they had ahead of them.

I love you.

Teague grinned. "I love you, too."

When they were both on their feet, Hudson took the rings and studied them. He noticed the inscription on the inside, and tears welled up in his eyes again. This man was going to forever surprise him, and for that, Hudson was more than grateful.

"So … where's my present?" Teague's tone was teasing.

Hudson glanced over at the man, smiled.

"What's that look for?" Teague questioned, sobering.

175

If the kid only knew.

CHAPTER

9

HIS NERVES HAD ABATED SOMEWHAT, WHICH WAS a good thing. After the proposal and Hudson's acceptance of it, they had walked down by the lake for a good hour, hand in hand, before they returned to the apartment. Teague figured Hudson knew how hard it was for him to be cooped up inside.

It was true. Teague had years of experience. He'd kept to himself, sharing his innermost secrets with no one, and certainly not sharing his space or his life. But now he had Hudson and everything had changed. For the better.

They made dinner together, ate together, then cleaned up together. Now that they were finished with all the mundane chores, Teague was beginning to feel restless again.

He tried to focus on the television, but it was doing nothing for him. Nothing on except Christmas movies that he had absolutely no interest in. Call him Scrooge or whatever, but this Christmas thing was still new to him. He was still getting used to the tree looming in the corner with its flashing lights and dangling ornaments. Oh, sure, he liked it, and he'd admitted as much to Hudson at some point, but he was ready for the holidays to be over. He wanted to get back to his regular routine; it was the only time he felt he could function normally.

Hudson snapped his fingers, and Teague glanced over to see him sitting on the couch, watching him.

"Huh?"

I didn't buy you anything for Christmas.

Teague laughed. "I'm okay with that." And he was. The whole present exchange was weird for him. He didn't want anything, didn't need anything, so gifts weren't necessary. He had everything he ever needed right here in this room with him.

Hudson's hands began to move again.

I am giving you myself for Christmas.

Teague chuckled. "How very generous of you."

Hudson didn't smile, his face serious.

Teague kept his eyes locked with Hudson's, trying to read between the lines here. Clearly Hudson was trying to tell him something.

I am giving myself to you. All of me. Whatever you want from me.

Again, Teague tried to comprehend, but he was coming up short.

Hudson shifted. *Tonight I belong to you. I am putting myself in your hands.*

Teague's eyes widened as he understood the implications of Hudson's words. "Oh … my … God."

Hudson nodded.

Teague's dick was already stirring to life. Then again, it usually did whenever Hudson talked to him.

"So, let's make sure we're both on the same page…" Teague cleared his throat. "You're gonna let me … top you?"

Honestly, Teague never thought he would see this day. Yes, it was his only remaining unfulfilled fantasy. Every other one, Hudson had fulfilled many times over. Even the spanking thing. Although until it happened, Teague hadn't been aware it was a fantasy of his. But topping Hudson…

Hudson nodded again.

Okay.

Yes.

Well.

Teague sucked air into his lungs as he continued to stare at the big guy. He could see the hesitancy on Hudson's face. Teague knew that no other man had ever had the pleasure of feeling Hudson beneath him, taking him in such an exquisitely intimate way.

Holy shit.

He wanted to jump the guy, to strip Hudson naked right there on the couch, to bury his dick so deep inside Hudson he didn't know anything else but what it felt like for Teague to claim him. The feeling was overwhelming with its intensity, yet somehow Teague managed to remain where he was.

If Hudson was going to give him this, then Teague was damn sure going to make it good for him.

And damn, wasn't this a new twist for him? He never thought about how Hudson took control so easily, how he commanded Teague's pleasure, rocked his fucking world. Yet he did, and Teague loved every minute of it.

The question was, how could he show Hudson just what this meant to him in the span of one night?

Hmmm.

He needed a plan.

HUDSON'S ENTIRE BODY WAS DRAWN TIGHT, HIS muscles tense, his nerves rioting. This was a first for him, and to be honest, he was terrified. Not that he would tell anyone that. No way would he let on that the kid freaked him out, and it had nothing to do with the fact that Teague would fuck him into oblivion. This wasn't about sex. Not entirely, anyway.

This was about giving himself completely to someone else. Teague seemed to do that freely, and Hudson took everything the kid offered him because he loved him. He thought nothing of it, but when the shoe was on the other foot...

It all came down to the fact that Hudson trusted Teague with his body. With his heart. With his soul. With his life. And yes, he wanted this. He wanted to share this with Teague, to feel him, to know what it meant to be completely invested in another person.

When Teague finally hopped up off the couch, Hudson's gaze trailed him, waiting with his heart in his throat.

Without a word, Teague came to stand in front of him, holding out his hand.

Hudson took it, praying the kid didn't realize how much he was shaking.

Teague led the way, muttering for Charger to stay as they headed across the hall to the other apartment. Rather than go straight to the bed, Teague continued into the bathroom. He flipped on the shower, then turned back to face Hudson.

"Relax," Teague whispered, his voice calm, gentle.

Hudson nodded, taking a deep breath, forcing the muscles in his shoulders to unknot.

When Teague pressed up against him, fusing their mouths, Hudson lost himself in the kiss. He felt Teague's hands as they slowly worked the button on his shorts free, lifted his shirt. Within minutes, they were both naked, tongues still seeking, and Hudson realized he had relaxed into the warmth of Teague's body. Somewhat.

He hadn't known what to expect from Teague, but then again, the kid was volatile. There was no way to predict what he would do next, but he seemed to realize how hard this was for Hudson. Another check mark in the *why I love him* column.

"Come on," Teague whispered, pulling Hudson's arm, urging him toward the shower.

The warm water cascaded over his back, his shoulders, sliding down his chest while Teague stood there, studying him. His blue eyes were intent as his hands slowly roamed over Hudson's chest.

"I won't hurt you," Teague promised. "I swear it."

Hudson nodded his head. He knew that. He had never doubted Teague for a second.

"Just let me love you. That's all I want to do."

Nodding, he decided then and there that he would stop thinking, stop worrying. This was the only place he wanted to be.

Hudson dropped his head back when Teague's mouth trailed over his chest. The man's teeth grazed Hudson's nipple, and he drew in a sharp breath as the sting vibrated through him, making his dick pulse. A firm hand wrapped around his shaft, gently stroking him.

He fought the urge to control, to dominate. It would be so easy to slide his fingers in Teague's hair, to force him to his knees, but he stopped himself short, wanting to let that all go.

"Turn around," Teague instructed, releasing him.

Hudson pivoted, planting his hands on the wall, ducking his head as the warm water poured over him.

Slippery hands slid over his skin, soaping him up as they moved. Teague's fingers were firm as they dug into the muscles of Hudson's neck, worked their way down. Hudson focused on the sensations, the incredible feeling stirring deep within him. The next thing he knew, the water had rinsed the suds from his body and Teague's hands had disappeared. He had to fight the urge to turn around, to see what Teague was doing. He didn't need to know. He trusted him.

Teague's warm mouth glided over his back, his tongue trailing the lines of his tattoos. Hudson drew air into his lungs in gulps as the incredible pleasure rocked him. And when Teague's tongue drifted down the crack of his ass, Hudson instinctively spread his legs, allowing for more of that mind-numbing feeling to course through his body.

It was clear Teague was taking his time, teasing, tormenting. Strong hands slid up his thighs, over his hips, back down to his cock, all while that devious tongue thrust into his ass, fucking him exquisitely, making his balls ache, his need ratcheting up another notch.

But then it was over, and he felt the loss of Teague's ministrations like a cold chill down his body. He wanted that warmth, needed to feel more of him.

"Go lie down on the bed. On your back," Teague instructed. "I'll be there in just a minute."

Hudson dried off, then slipped out of the bathroom to do as Teague instructed.

And for the first time since he'd made his proclamation earlier, a smile curved the corners of his lips as he thought about what was to come.

CHAPTER 10

SEX WAS SOMETHING TEAGUE WAS INTIMATELY FAMILIAR with. It wasn't a secret that he'd been a little more than promiscuous in his lifetime. Safe, but promiscuous nonetheless. It had always been about the physical release. He'd purposely kept emotions out of it.

But when it came to Hudson, this was a whole new world for him. Every single time they were together was like the first time for him. Teague trusted the man implicitly, knew Hudson was going to take care of him.

In turn, Teague wanted to take care of Hudson.

Which was why he'd moved the events to their bed. After sending Hudson on his way, Teague washed up, brushed his teeth, and stood there, staring at himself in the mirror. No doubt about it, he was a different man than he'd been a year ago. A better man. One who had experienced things he'd never imagined possible. His heart didn't merely send blood pumping through his body these days, it now belonged to someone.

Taking a deep breath, Teague stepped out of the bedroom, mentally steeling himself for what he would find.

There was Hudson, lying on the bed, spread-eagled, looking like a holiday feast.

Yeah, this was the type of Christmas meal he could get used to.

He watched Hudson's face as his gaze trailed over him, head to toe, back up again. There was a hunger in Hudson's eyes, one that mirrored what was inside Teague as he calmly perused the sexy beast laid out before him.

Teague crawled onto the bed, pressing his lips to Hudson's shins. First one, then the other. He slowly kissed his way higher, over the man's thick, muscular thighs, stopping where his leg met his hip. He savored every taste, cherished every inhale of Hudson's musky scent. He could get used to this.

Allowing his breath to fan over Hudson's cock, Teague slid his hands over Hudson's chest, feeling the steady throb of Hudson's pulse throughout his body.

Knowing Hudson had a tremendous amount of self-control, Teague didn't worry that he would try to dominate him. The man had handed himself over, placed himself in Teague's care, and he wanted nothing more than to take Hudson up on his offer, to enjoy every minute of this.

Of course, Teague had to deal with the fact that he had very little patience himself. He could only tease and be teased for so long before the need became an urgent vibration within him, his body demanding more.

Working his way up Hudson's body, Teague found Hudson's mouth and claimed it with his own. Kissing, searching. When Hudson's hands wrapped around him, the warmth enveloping his entire body, Teague groaned his pleasure. He loved this, every single thing about it.

"My dick's so hard it hurts," he whispered to Hudson. "It's all you. You make me hard, make me desperate."

Teague managed to pull back, kneeling between Hudson's thighs after he retrieved the lube from the nightstand.

"Pull your knees up," he instructed. "Let me see that sweet ass of yours."

Hudson did as he was told, his knees wide. It left the man exposed, and Teague watched the emotions flash in the emerald green of his eyes. Vulnerability warring with desire, uncertainty battling with need.

"I'm not gonna hurry," he warned Hudson. "Once I'm inside you, I plan to take my time with you."

Approval flickered in Hudson's gaze.

After applying a generous amount of lube, Teague leaned over Hudson, forcing his legs even higher as he guided himself into the warmth of the man's body. His lungs ceased to function as the heat overwhelmed him.

"Tight," he groaned through clenched teeth, leaning over Hudson, wanting his mouth.

Teague kissed him as he pushed in deep, feeling Hudson's muscles tighten.

"Fuck…" Teague had been serious when he said he wanted to take his time, but jeezus fuck, that was a hell of a lot harder than he anticipated. "Relax, Hudson. Let it feel good."

Rocking his hips, Teague found Hudson's mouth with his own, kissing him slowly, deeply. He savored every single second he was with this man, his heart full to bursting as he took what Hudson so freely gave him.

Hudson's hand gripped Teague's ass, pulling him, forcing him deeper inside. He tried to keep a slow, steady rhythm, but his dick ached for the friction that Hudson's body could provide.

He forced himself back, on his knees once again, still lodged deep.

"Need to watch as I fuck you," he explained.

Teague's eyes locked on the point where their bodies were joined, his dick sliding in, retreating. Minutes ticked by as he remained fascinated, completely overcome by incredible emotions. He'd always preferred to be the bottom, to have a man dominate him. And when it came to Hudson, Teague found he still wanted that. Even after this, after the pleasure he'd never known existed, he couldn't help but want it.

While he continued to rock forward and back, filling Hudson, withdrawing, Teague found the lube, poured a liberal amount on Hudson's cock. He stroked him, working him up, preparing him. And when it was clear that Hudson was close, Teague pulled out of him and repositioned Hudson's legs so that they were straight out, allowing Teague to inch forward so that he could take Hudson's cock into his ass.

Wide green eyes stared back at him as Teague eased down on Hudson's shaft.

"Oh, fuck yes," he hissed, holding Hudson's stare. "This is what I want. This is what I always want, Hudson. You. Inside me."

As much as he'd wanted to be the one in control, Teague knew that this was where he was meant to be. Where he belonged.

Right here.

Just like this.

HUDSON WAS ON THE VERGE OF COMING so hard he was almost certain his brain would explode. Feeling Teague inside him... Goddamn, it had been better than he'd ever thought it could be. The way Teague had seen to his pleasure, taken care of him.

But now, as Teague lifted and lowered on his cock, Hudson knew this was how they were meant to be. He could see it in the way Teague looked at him. The kid needed this. So did Hudson.

"As much as I've enjoyed this," Teague whispered, "I need more. I need you."

Hudson knew exactly what he meant. In one effortless move, he forced Teague onto his back, coming over him, then lodging himself deep once again. He linked his fingers with Teague's, held them over his head, and began pumping his hips, the motions synchronizing with the pounding of his heart.

"Oh, yeah... This is what I want, Hudson. This. Forever. You inside me. You loving me. Showing me how much."

If he could only tell Teague with words, he would. Since that wasn't possible and they both knew it, Hudson held Teague's gaze, making sure he knew everything he felt. And for the first time in his life, he mouthed words, wanting to ensure Teague understood: *I love you.* Clearly he took Teague by surprise, the man's eyes widening, so much love reflecting back at him. Then Hudson kissed him. Hard. Deep. He thrust his tongue into Teague's mouth as he thrust his cock deep into Teague's ass.

The torrent of sensation made it hard to breathe; the sheer ecstasy of being with this man assaulted his body, his mind, his soul. It was all he needed, all he wanted.

Teague rocked beneath him, moaning into his mouth. The kid was close; Hudson knew he was. Then again, so was he. There was no holding back as sensations ripped through him, stealing what air was left in his lungs as his balls tightened, his dick pulsing.

And when Teague cried out, the sound muffled by Hudson's mouth, they both came in a rush, their bodies plastered together, hearts entwined, worlds colliding.

It took several minutes for Hudson to get his breathing under control. Only then did he disappear into the bathroom to clean up, returning with a warm cloth to clean Teague.

"I can't move," Teague mumbled. "I think you broke me."

Hudson grinned and kissed Teague gently.

"Until tomorrow, that is," Teague added. "Tomorrow I'll be as good as new, and if Santa wants to bring me more of that, I'm game."

Santa, huh?

Hmm.

Hudson could probably get on board with that plan.

CHAPTER 11

Sunday, December 25

"I HOPE YOU KNOW, YOU'RE MAKING THIS up to me later," Teague mumbled as Hudson pulled down Cam and Gannon's street, getting closer and closer to this inevitable Christmas dinner.

Hudson didn't respond. Then again, he was driving.

Or perhaps he didn't respond because he didn't want to. Teague *had* been bitching about it since they'd woken up this morning. Even after Hudson had introduced him to the gift that Santa had brought. The guy was ridiculously creative, and he'd shown it when he padded into the living room with Teague in tow, both of them completely naked. It was then that Hudson had fucked him like a madman right there on the floor in front of the Christmas tree, the lights twinkling over their naked bodies. Needless to say, Teague had a newfound appreciation for Christmas.

However, it was his civic duty to give the man a hard time if he insisted on forcing Teague to do things that were out of his comfort zone.

Like having dinner with people.

In another effort to irritate Hudson, Teague stared at him. He didn't look away once as the big guy brought the truck to a stop against the curb in front of the quaint little house that Cam and Gannon occupied. When Hudson glanced over, Teague grinned. How could he not?

You will be fine.

"Or so you say." Teague took a deep breath. "I've been thinking about us getting married."

Hudson lifted his hand, did that rolling motion that urged Teague to continue.

"I'd like to do it soon. Do you think we could get a marriage license tomorrow? Then maybe get married on the second?"

He would've suggested they get married on the first, but he knew it was a holiday.

Of January?

Teague nodded.

Hudson reached over and grabbed Teague's neck, pulling him to him. The kiss the man planted on him was one hell of a yes, or so Teague hoped.

"So we can avoid telling everyone?"

Not a chance.

Teague pouted. "Fine. But I get to be the one to do it."

Hudson's eyebrow lifted.

Teague grinned. "What? Is it wrong that I want everyone to know that I've trapped you and you're willing to marry me? Come on. I'm so going to exploit this."

Hudson shook his head in disbelief, making Teague laugh.

Without waiting for a response, Teague hurried out of the truck, then let Charger out of the back seat before heading up to the house with Hudson at his side.

They rang the doorbell and waited.

When Milly appeared on the other side of the door, Teague grinned.

"Y'all made it."

"We're getting married," Teague blurted, then hurried past her as she giggled.

Once inside, Teague removed his coat, turning to see Hudson looking at him.

I thought you wanted to tell everyone.

"I do. That's why I told Milly first. She'll make sure everyone knows in five … four … three … two…"

"They're getting married!" Milly yelled from the living room. "Teague did it! He popped the question."

Teague grinned.

Sometimes this shit was just too easy.

CHAPTER 12

Monday, January 2

HUDSON HADN'T EXPECTED TO BE EDGY, BUT that was exactly how he found himself. He'd been fine for the past few days, but as of this morning, he felt twitchy, nervous.

Getting a marriage license, waiting the allotted seventy-two hours, then getting an appointment with the Justice of the Peace… All of that was easy. But showing up here, waiting for their turn before the judge who would officially marry them was going to make Hudson go gray. Possibly before they left the building.

"Relax, big guy," Teague whispered. "It's no different than giving yourself up to me." Teague grinned. "And you did great that night. Then again, this is forever, and technically, you are giving yourself to me for all time. So…"

Hudson scowled. He wasn't doubting his desire to marry this man. He just wished it was over already so they could go back to the apartment and Hudson could dominate his husband.

Husband.

He fucking loved the sound of that.

Loved it.

Just thinking it made his heart swell and his gut churn.

It took a tremendous amount of effort to remember to breathe.

Several minutes later, they were called into a room where a judge stood waiting for them. A lady, presumably the witness for the ceremony, was following them after she closed the door.

The room was a simple courtroom. Nothing fancy.

The woman handed the judge the marriage license, and he looked it over, then looked up at the two of them with a smile on his face.

A smile.

A real one.

Honestly, Hudson hadn't known what to expect. Although gay marriage was now legal, he knew that there was a lot of opposition to it. Not only in Texas but everywhere. The fact that this man could make him feel welcome allowed Hudson to breathe a little easier.

"Are you gentlemen ready?" the man asked.

Teague looked at Hudson, then back at the judge. "Sir, I'd like to let you know that he's mute. He cannot repeat what you say, but he will sign it for me. If that's all right with you."

The judge met Hudson's eyes. "That's perfect."

The next five minutes were a blur. Hudson's pulse had pounded painfully hard, his blood roaring in his head as they exchanged their vows and the rings. Of course, Hudson did remember trying to put Teague's ring on the wrong finger. Twice.

Thankfully, the kid had been ready for everything, clearly handling this far better than Hudson was. Which was a first.

"I now pronounce you husband and husband. You may kiss," the man stated, looking pleased.

Teague turned toward him and Hudson's heart leapt into his throat.

He had every intention of grabbing Teague and kissing him hard, but the next thing he knew, Teague was the one initiating it, taking charge.

And it was in that very moment, as he kissed the man he could now call his husband, that Hudson realized something.

Hudson hadn't been the one to save Teague, despite how it had all played out. It had been the opposite, really. Teague had saved him in so many ways. He'd given him a love that would withstand anything.

191

And on this day, the second day of the new year, the man married him.

Hudson seriously doubted there would ever be a better start to a new year again.

I HOPE YOU ENJOYED HUDSON & TEAGUE. To be honest, these are two of my absolute favorite characters. They are a proper balance, and I enjoy every second I get to spend with them.

Read more about the characters you saw in this book:

Reckless (Cam & Gannon)

Fearless (Dare & Noah)

Speechless (Hudson & Teague)

Harmless (Roan & Seg)

You can find all of Nicole's books at the back of this book or on her website: www.NicoleEdwards.me

Letters to Curtis & Lorrie

Dear reader,

Earlier this year, I released *Curtis*, the first book in The Walkers of Coyote Ridge series. If you've read about the Walker brothers, then you are familiar with their mom & dad. Well, Curtis and Lorrie's story takes place from the beginning. You get to see how they met, how their love developed, turning into a lifetime of love. And to celebrate that release, I had each of the brothers write a letter to their parents. These were posted on my blog. I hope you enjoy!

Much love,

Nicole Edwards

DEAR MOM & POP,

SO, I'M SURE MY BROTHERS HAVE REMINDED YOU OF ALL THE MISCHIEVOUS THINGS THEY'VE DONE, BUT I'M ALSO BETTING THEY LEFT OUT ALL THE THINGS THEY DID THAT THEY BLAMED ON ME. IN MY DEFENSE, I AM THE YOUNGEST, AND I HAD SIX OLDER BROTHERS WHO MOLDED ME INTO WHAT YOU THOUGHT WAS A TROUBLEMAKER.

SURE, I CAN NAME A COUPLE OF TIMES WHEN I MIGHT HAVE BEEN AT FAULT. LIKE THE TIME I STOLE A WHOLE DISPLAY OF GUM FROM THE STORE, AND WHEN MOM FOUND IT, I TOLD HER BEAU DID IT. OF COURSE, MOM TOLD ME SHE CALLED THE POLICE ON BEAU AND THAT THEY WERE GOING TO TAKE HIM TO JAIL. I EVENTUALLY CONFESSED BECAUSE I COULDN'T HAVE BEAU GOING TO JAIL FOR MY CRIME. SO, NOT ALL BAD.

AND MAYBE THE TIME WHEN SAWYER AND TRAVIS WERE HELPING POP FIX SOMETHING ON THE ROOF, AND I STOLE THE LADDER AND WOULDN'T BRING IT BACK.

THOSE WERE MINOR THINGS, THOUGH. I CAN THINK OF OTHERS THAT WEREN'T MY FAULT.

FOR EXAMPLE, WHAT ABOUT THE TIME WHEN KALEB PUT MY BICYCLE IN THE TREE? I THINK HE SAID SOMETHING ABOUT ME LEAVING IT IN FRONT OF THE DOOR, AND HE TRIPPED OVER IT OR SOMETHING. (I DOUBT THAT WAS TRUE.) I HAD TO GET POP TO GET IT DOWN FOR ME. KALEB'S FAULT.

OR WHAT ABOUT THE TIME WHEN ETHAN CONVINCED ME THAT ELEVATORS WERE GOING TO EAT ME AND THAT IF I EVER GOT IN ONE, I'D NEVER GET BACK OUT. WE HAD TO TAKE THE STAIRS FOR A WHILE AFTER THAT. ETHAN'S FAULT.

ALSO, THE TIME WHEN BRAYDON AND BRENDON PUT THE SNOW MACHINE IN THE SCHOOL CAFETERIA. I TOOK THE BLAME FOR THAT ONE. THEN AGAIN, THAT WAS A BRILLIANT IDEA. STILL, THAT WAS THE TWINS' FAULT, NOT MINE.

AND THE TIME SAWYER CONVINCED ME THAT I HAD POISON IVY AND THE ONLY WAY TO GET RID OF IT WAS TO COVER MYSELF IN CALADRYL LOTION AND NOT WEAR CLOTHES. I WAS PINK. AND NAKED. IT JUST SO HAPPENED TO BE THE DAY THAT THE LADIES FROM CHURCH WERE COMING OVER FOR LUNCH. THAT WAS SAWYER'S FAULT.

TRUTH IS, THEY WERE THE TROUBLEMAKERS AND I WAS THE SCAPEGOAT. YEP, THAT'S MY STORY AND I'M STICKING TO IT. BUT DON'T WORRY, I FULLY INTEND TO CORRUPT MY NIECES AND NEPHEWS TO PAY MY BROTHERS BACK FOR ALL THE DAMAGE THEY DID.

LOVE YOU TONS,
YOUR FAVORITE SON, ZANE

Dear Mom & Pop,

I'm going to start this out by saying that I was the good kid. The quiet kid. The one who didn't get into anything. Yes, I'm smiling while I write this. And no, maybe I wasn't the quiet one, but I wanted you to believe that I was. And sometimes it worked.

I think you'll remember the time when I was going to build the biggest, best fire in the fireplace. Before I started (and roped Zane into helping me), I asked permission. So, I did it the right way. However, no one told me that I couldn't keep adding wood, so technically it wasn't really my fault. But, aside from nearly burning down the house, the best part was when Pop got irritated at the smoke detector and, rather than trying to put out the fire (which was definitely getting out of control), he was more worried about making the alarm stop. That was the greatest.

Oh, and I'm thankful I didn't burn down the house. I'm sure you are too. And thank you for continuing to love us, no matter what damage we did. Love you!

Love,
Ethan

Dear Mom & Pop,

It's sometimes hard to think back on all the things we did as kids, all the trouble we caused. But that's only because I forget which was my fault and which was Brendon's. For the record, most of it was Brendon. I was the good twin and he was a bad influence. (I know you believe that)

There are two big things I remember. The first was the time when Brendon and I decided to have a Roman candle fight in the backyard. You remember that, right? When we used metal trashcan lids as our shields, and shot the fireworks directly at one another. I think we were thirteen. God, that was fun. It was a wonder we didn't burn down the barn.

And what about the time when he and I got in a towel fight? It started out we were popping each other. When we grew bored of that, we soaked the bath towels and threw them at each other. In the house. I remember Pop sitting in his recliner, yelling at us. He finally stopped hollering, so we kept right on going. Then the minute Mom walked in the door, we knew we were in for it. I think there are still water spots on the ceiling from that day.

Yep, I think it's safe to say that the two of you've earned the Parents of the Century award for all that you've endured over the years. But through it all, you managed not to throttle us. Sometimes, I'm not sure how. Love you guys!

Love,
Braydon

Dear Mom & Pop,

When Nicole asked me to come up with a memorable moment, I have to say, I was worried. Only because I wasn't sure I could think of just one. There are so many great ones to choose from. But, I'm curious, which one is your favorite?

I remember the time when Braydon wouldn't give me something that I wanted. We were like six at the time. I kept pulling him around by his arm until I pulled it right out of the socket. Of course, I felt bad at the time, but the funny part came when he couldn't walk because of it. His injury had nothing to do with his legs, but for some reason, he thought he couldn't walk. Luckily, the doctor got that sucker right back where it belonged and his legs worked again. Ha!

Or, what about the time when I carved Braydon's name into the bathroom counter? Remember that? I wanted him to get in trouble. Wait, now that I think about it, maybe you didn't know that was me. Never mind. That was really Braydon.

Regardless of all the crap we put you through, I hope you know how much we love you. Me especially. I love you the most.

Love,
Brendon

Dear Mom & Pop,

Let's just say that I hope Mason and Kellan don't figure out a fraction of what we did as kids. I have to give you guys props for managing to keep us in line as much as you did. I can remember so many times when Pop was ready to string us up by our shoelaces. Fun times!

I think the time I remember most was shortly after Pop had finished painting the kitchen. I remember wanting to help, but he told me I'd have to wait until I was a little bit older. He said the paintbrush was too big for me. So, rather than argue, I fished out Mom's fingernail polish and proceeded to paint the wall in my bedroom. And the carpet. And my leg. I then invited you both to come check out the masterpiece.

Something I might've left out of that story was the fact that Sawyer showed me where the fingernail polish was. He even helped me to pick out which colors to use.

Sometimes I wonder how y'all made it.

Love,
Kaleb

Dear Mom & Pop,

I wish I could say that all of the stunts I pulled happened as a kid, but we'd all know that wasn't true. I'm sure you remember the signs because... Well, because those moments are definitely unforgettable.

However, when I think back to my childhood, there are a couple of moments that definitely require some reminiscing. Like the time I shot my BB gun in the house, and I actually shot a hole through the refrigerator. You have to give me credit because you didn't actually find that one until months later. That magnet, combined with Travis's report card, worked quite well at covering up the crime scene.

Or how about the time when I decided I was going to go live with Grandma? I packed my bag, hopped on my tricycle, and y'all let me get at least a mile away before Pops came and picked me up, set me and my tricycle in the bed of the truck, and brought me back home. The best part was when he got me out, put me on the ground, and I took off again. Thought I'd teach him. Funny how I was the only one of us who was out of breath.

Lots of fond memories, Mom & Pop. I thank you for every one of them. Love you both!

Love,
Sawyer

Dear Mom & Pop,

While I sit here trying to think of all the crazy stunts we pulled as kids, I think of so many things. I've shared these stories with Kylie and Gage a few times as well and I always get the same looks. The one that says, "I don't doubt that at all." You'd think we were rowdy or something.

The one thing I remember most is back when Sawyer was in kindergarten (maybe first grade) and we both had to stay home from school because we were sick. I convinced him that the police were going to come get us because we were skipping school and since it was illegal to skip school, we needed to hide.

Well, technically, I told him that *he* needed to hide. You were quite upset with me at the time because he fell asleep in the dryer and I forgot about him.

Now that I think about it, I guess it was a good thing I hadn't turned it on.

AND YES, I KNOW WE CAUSED YOU TO PULL YOUR HAIR OUT FROM ALL THE CRAP WE PULLED, AND NOW THAT I'VE GOT A RAMBUNCTIOUS RUGRAT OF MY OWN, I FEEL YOUR PAIN. I ALSO LOVE YOU FOR IT.

LOVE,
TRAVIS

Stay Tuned

This was my first year doing this, and I have to say, it was so much fun. It took far less time to get pulled back into the stories than I thought it would. I hope you enjoyed spending the holidays with them as I did.

If you enjoyed *Naughty Holidays 2016*, please consider leaving a review.

Acknowledgments

While writing is a solitary task, it's not a completely solo project. Because of that, I'd like to thank those who've assisted in one way or another.

As a side note, I received no compensation for these acknowledgments, so they are in no particular order.

My characters: I'd like to thank you all for making such an impression that you stuck with me long after your story was written.

You, the reader: I'm humbled that you wanted more. Two years running. So thank you. Thank you for reading, thank you for writing a review, and thank you for hopping on social media and telling your friends about the book. You're magnificent like that.

ABOUT NICOLE EDWARDS

New York Times and *USA Today* bestselling author Nicole Edwards spends her days stringing words together to make complete sentences. Sometimes not. Her best friend is coffee, and she has a love/hate relationship with sarcasm. She's been accused of having a filthy imagination, which she admits is true.

Nicole lives in the suburbs of Austin, Texas. She proudly claims one husband, three grown children, and three bosses (better known as the dogs). When she isn't writing, watching football or hockey, or keeping her bosses happy, you can probably find her with a book in hand.

BEFORE YOU GO!

Now that you've read one of my books, I'd like to think we can consider ourselves friends. And since friends usually hang out, I want to let you know where you can find me.

If you've got a minute or two, I hope you'll visit my website - **www.NicoleEdwards.me** - to find exclusive content you won't find anywhere else, including my Ramblings of a Writer Blog, Sneak Peeks, the Walker Family Tree, A Day in the Life character stories, exclusive giveaways, and more. If you'd like to be part of the VIP crowd, you can join Nicole Nation (free and easy to do) and get access to more cool stuff, like the option to join my review team if you're so inclined.

Don't forget to sign up for **Nic News** … This is my newsletter, a.k.a. where the good stuff is. The best part: it's sent directly to your inbox. And because I know how difficult it is to manage your email, you've got a couple of options. When you sign up, you can choose to get the bare minimum: announcements for preorders and new releases. Or you can go all in and get those plus fun stuff like the Nic Newsflash, as well as giveaways, sales, etc. Either way you go, I only send out a couple a month, so I promise not to spam your email.

Oh, and I can't forget my **Naughty & Nice Shop**! This is where you'll find signed books and fun merch. There's plenty of naughty and nice options to go around.

Last but not least, if you're on Facebook, you should check out my reader group: **Nicole Nation**. This is where I interact with my friends. You can ask me questions, play fun weekly games, celebrate during release week, and enter exclusive giveaways!

You can also follow me on:

Facebook
/Author.Nicole.Edwards

Instagram
/NicoleEdwardsAuthor

TikTok
/@nicoleedwardsauthor

BookBub
/NicoleEdwardsAuthor

By Nicole Edwards

THE WALKERS OF COYOTE RIDGE
Kaleb

Zane

Travis

Holidays with The Walker Brothers

Ethan

Braydon

Sawyer

Brendon

Curtis

Jared

Hard to Hold

Hard to Handle

Beau

Rex

A Coyote Ridge Christmas

Mack

Kaden & Keegan

Trey

Rafe

Violet

BRANTLEY WALKER: OFF THE BOOKS
All In
Without A Trace
Hide & Seek
Deadly Coincidence
Alibi
Secrets
Confessions
Bounty
Off Course
Chain Reaction
To Have and To Hold
Missing Pieces
Smoke and Mirrors

THE JAMESONS OF COYOTE RIDGE
Hot Chocolate Wishes
Rough & Dirty

AUSTIN ARROWS
Rush
Kaufman

CLUB DESTINY
Conviction
Temptation
Addicted
Seduction
Infatuation
Captivated
Devotion
Perception
Entrusted
Adored
Distraction
Forevermore

DEAD HEAT RANCH
Boots Optional

Betting on Grace

Overnight Love

Jared *(a crossover novel)*

DEVIL'S BEND
Chasing Dreams

Vanishing Dreams

MISPLACED HALOS
Protected in Darkness

Salvation in Darkness

Bound in Darkness

OFFICE INTRIGUE
Office Intrigue

Intrigued Out of The Office

Their Rebellious Submissive

Their Famous Dominant

Their Ruthless Sadist

Their Naughty Student

Their Fairy Princess

Owned

PIER 70
Reckless

Fearless

Speechless

Harmless

Clueless

PRIMAL INSTINCTS
Chase (Volume 1-3)

Capture (Volume 4-6)

Claim (Volume 7-9)

HEROES & HAVOC
(Sniper 1 Security, Devil's Playground, Southern Boy Mafia)

Wait for Morning
Beautifully Brutal
Without Regret
Never Say Never
Beautifully Loyal
Without Restraint
Tomorrow's Too Late

STANDALONE NOVELS
Unhinged Trilogy
A Million Tiny Pieces
Inked on Paper
Bad Reputation
Bad Business
Filthy Hot Billionaire
RULE

NAUGHTY HOLIDAY EDITIONS
2015
2016
2021